THE

A STORY BY DAVID HERBERT LAWRENCE

MAN

WITH A SUITE OF WOODCUTS BY LEONARD BASKIN

WHO

AND A COMMENTARY BY JOHN FOWLES

DIED

THE ECCO PRESS

The Ecco Press
100 West Broad Street
Hopewell, NJ 08525
Published simultaneously in Canada by
Penguin Books Canada Ltd., Ontario
Printed in the United States of America

Library of Congress Cataloging-in-Publication Data

Lawrence, D. H. (David Herbert), 1885–1930.
The man who died : a story / by David Herbert Lawrence ; with a suite of woodcuts
by Leonard Baskin ; and a commentary by John Fowles.
p.   cm.
1. Jesus Christ—Fiction. 2. Bible. N.T.—History of Biblical events—Fiction. I. Title
PR6023.A93M27   1994
823'.914—dc20   93-39307
ISBN 0-88001-353-2
ISBN 0-88001-429-6 paperback

The text of this book is set in Bembo

9 8 7 6 5 4 3 2 1

FIRST ECCO PAPERBACK EDITION

THE
MAN
WHO
DIED

PART ONE

There was a peasant near Jerusalem who acquired a young gamecock which looked a shabby little thing, but which put on brave feathers as spring advanced and was resplendent with arched and orange neck by the time the fig trees were letting out leaves from their end tips.

This peasant was poor, he lived in a cottage of mud-brick, and had only a dirty little inner courtyard with a tough fig-tree for all his territory. He worked hard among the vines and olives and wheat of his master, then came home to sleep in the mud-brick cottage by the path. But he was proud of his young rooster. In the shut-in yard were three shabby hens which laid small eggs, shed the few feathers they had, and made a disproportionate amount of dirt. There was also, in a corner under a straw roof, a dull donkey that often went out with the peasant to work, but sometimes stayed at home. And there was the peasant's wife, a black-browed youngish woman who did not work too hard. She threw a little grain, or the remains of the porridge mess, to the fowls, and she cut green fodder with a sickle, for the ass.

The young cock grew to a certain splendour. By some freak of destiny, he was a dandy rooster, in that dirty little yard with three patchy hens. He learned to crane his neck and give shrill answers to the crowing of other cocks, beyond the walls, in a world he knew nothing of. But there was a special fiery colour to his crow, and the distant calling of the other cocks roused him to unexpected outbursts.

"How he sings," said the peasant, as he got up and pulled his day-shirt over his head.

"He is good for twenty hens," said the wife.

The peasant went out and looked with pride at his young rooster. A saucy, flamboyant bird that has already made the final acquaintance of the three tattered hens. But the cockerel was tipping his head, listening to the challenge of far-off unseen cocks, in the unknown world. Ghost voices, crowing at him mysteriously out of limbo. He answered with a ringing defiance, never to be daunted.

"He will surely fly away one of these days," said the peasant's wife.

So they lured him with grain, caught him, though he fought with all his wings and feet, and they tied a cord round his shank, fastening it against the spur; and they tied the other end of the cord to the post that held up the donkey's straw pent-roof.

The young cock, freed, marched with a prancing stride of indignation away from the humans, came to the end of his string, gave a tug and a hitch of his tied leg, fell over for a moment, scuffled frantically on the unclean earthen floor, to the horror of the shabby hens, then with a sickening lurch, regained his feet, and stood to think. The peasant and the peasant's wife laughed heartily, and the young cock heard them. And he knew, with a gloomy, foreboding kind of knowledge, that he was tied by the leg.

He no longer pranced and ruffled and forged his feathers. He walked within the limits of his tether sombrely. Still he gobbled up the best bits of food. Still, sometimes, he saved an extra-best bit for his favourite hen of the moment. Still he pranced with quivering, rocking fierceness

4

upon such of his harem as came nonchalantly within range, and gave off the invisible lure. And still he crowed defiance to the cock-crows that showered up out of limbo, in the dawn.

But there was now a grim voracity in the way he gobbled his food, and a pinched triumph in the way he seized upon the shabby hens. His voice, above all, had lost the full gold of its clangour. He was tied by the leg and he knew it. Body, soul and spirit were tied by that string.

Underneath, however, the life in him was grimly unbroken. It was the cord that should break. So one morning, just before the light of dawn, rousing from his slumbers with a sudden wave of strength, he leaped forward on his wings, and the string snapped. He gave a wild strange squawk, rose in one lift to the top of the wall, and there he crowed a loud and splitting crow. So loud, it woke the peasant.

At the same time, at the same hour before dawn, on the same morning, a man awoke from a long sleep in which he was tied up. He woke numb and cold, inside a carved hole in the rock. Through all the long sleep his body had been full of hurt, and it was still full of hurt. He did not open his eyes. Yet he knew that he was awake, and numb, and cold, and rigid, and full of hurt, and tied up. His face was banded with cold bands, his legs were bandaged together. Only his hands were loose.

He could move if he wanted: he knew that. But he had no want. Who would want to come back from the dead? A deep, deep nausea stirred in him, at the premonition of movement. He resented already the fact of the strange, incalculable moving that had already taken place in him: the moving back into consciousness. He had not wished it. He had wanted to stay outside, in the place where even memory is stone dead.

5

But now, something had returned to him, like a returned letter, and in that return he lay overcome with a sense of nausea. Yet suddenly his hands moved. They lifted up, cold, heavy and sore. Yet they lifted up, to drag away the cloth from his face, and to push at the shoulder bands. Then they fell again, cold, heavy, numb, and sick with having moved even so much, unspeakably unwilling to move further.

With his face cleared, and his shoulders free, he lapsed again, and lay dead, resting on the cold nullity of being dead. It was the most desirable. And almost, he had it complete: the utter cold nullity of being outside.

Yet when he was most nearly gone, suddenly, driven by an ache at the wrists, his hands rose and began pushing at the bandages of his knees, his feet began to stir, even while his breast lay cold and dead still.

And at last, the eyes opened. On to the dark. The same dark! yet perhaps there was a pale chink, of the all-disturbing light, prizing open the pure dark. He could not lift his head. The eyes closed. And again it was finished.

Then suddenly he leaned up, and the great world reeled. Bandages fell away. And narrow walls of rock closed upon him, and gave the new anguish of imprisonment. There were chinks of light. With a wave of strength that came from revulsion, he leaned forward, in that narrow well of rock, and leaned frail hands on the rock near the chinks of light.

Strength came from somewhere, from revulsion; there was a crash and a wave of light, and the dead man was crouching in his lair, facing the animal onrush of light. Yet it was hardly dawn. And the strange, piercing keenness of daybreak's sharp breath was on him. It meant full awakening.

6

Slowly, slowly he crept down from the cell of rock, with the caution of the bitterly wounded. Bandages and linen and perfume fell away, and he crouched on the ground against the wall of rock, to recover oblivion. But he saw his hurt feet touching the earth again, with unspeakable pain, the earth they had meant to touch no more, and he saw his thin legs that had died, and pain unknowable, pain like utter bodily disillusion, filled him so full that he stood up, with one torn hand on the ledge of the tomb.

To be back! To be back again, after all that! He saw the linen swathing-bands fallen round his dead feet, and stooping, he picked them up, folded them, and laid them back in the rocky cavity from which he had emerged. Then he took the perfumed linen sheet, wrapped it round him as a mantle, and turned away, to the wanness of the chill dawn.

He was alone; and having died, was even beyond loneliness.

Filled still with the sickness of unspeakable disillusion, the man stepped with wincing feet down the rocky slope, past the sleeping soldiers, who lay wrapped in their woollen mantles under the wild laurels. Silent, on naked scarred feet, wrapped in a white linen shroud, he glanced down for a moment on the inert, heap-like bodies of the soldiers. They were repulsive, a slow squalor of limbs, yet he felt a certain compassion. He passed on towards the road, lest they should wake.

Having nowhere to go, he turned from the city that stood on her hills. He slowly followed the road away from the town, past the olives, under which purple anemones were drooping in the chill of dawn, and rich-green herbage was pressing thick. The world, the same as ever, the natural world, thronging with greenness, a nightingale winsomely, wistfully, coaxingly calling from the bushes beside a runnel of water, in the world, the natural world of morning and evening, forever undying, from which he had died.

He went on, on scarred feet, neither of this world nor of the next. Neither here nor there, neither seeing nor yet sightless, he passed dimly on, away from the city and its precincts, wondering why he should be travelling, yet driven by a dim, deep nausea of disillusion, and a resolution of which he was not even aware.

Advancing in a kind of half-consciousness under the dry stone wall of the olive orchard, he was roused by the shrill wild crowing of a cock just near him, a sound which made him shiver as if electricity had touched him. He saw a black and orange cock on a bough above the road, then running through the olives of the upper level, a peasant in a grey woollen shirt-tunic. Leaping out of greenness, came the black and orange cock with the red comb, his tail-feathers streaming lustrous.

"O stop him, Master!" called the peasant. "My escaped cock!"

The man addressed, with a sudden flicker of smile, opened his great white wings of a shroud in front of the leaping bird. The cock fell back with a squawk and a flutter, the peasant jumped forward, there was a terrific beating of wings, and whirring of feathers, then the peasant had the escaped cock safely under his arm, its wings shut down, its face crazily craning forward, its round eyes goggling from its white chops.

"It's my escaped cock!" said the peasant, soothing the bird with his left hand, as he looked perspiringly up into the face of the man wrapped in white linen.

The peasant changed countenance, and stood transfixed, as he looked into the dead-white face of the man who had died. That dead-white face, so still, with the black beard growing on it as if in death; and those wide-open black sombre eyes, that had died! and those washed scars on the waxy forehead! The slow-blooded man of the field let his jaw drop, in childish inability to meet the situation.

"Don't be afraid," said the man in the shroud. "I am not dead. They took me down too soon. So I have risen up. Yet if they discover me, they will do it all over again. . . ."

He spoke in a voice of old disgust. Humanity! Especially humanity in authority! There was only one thing it could do. He looked with black, indifferent eyes into the quick shifty eyes of the peasant. The peasant quailed, and was powerless under the look of deathly indifference, and strange cold resoluteness. He could only say the one thing he was afraid to say:

"Will you hide in my house, Master?"

"I will rest there. But if you tell anyone, you know what will happen. You will have to go before a judge."

"Me! I shan't speak. Let us be quick!"

The peasant looked round in fear, wondering sulkily why he had let himself in for this doom. The man with scarred feet climbed painfully up to the level of the olive garden, and followed the sullen, hurrying peasant across the green wheat among the olive trees. He felt the cool silkiness of the young wheat under his feet that had been dead, and the roughishness of its separate life was apparent to him. At the edges of rocks, he saw the silky, silvery-haired buds of the scarlet anemone bending downwards. And they too were in another world. In his own world he was alone, utterly alone. These things around him were in a world that had never died. But he himself had died, or had been killed from out of it, and all that remained now was the great void nausea of utter disillusion.

They came to a clay cottage, and the peasant waited dejectedly for the other man to pass.

"Pass!" he said. "Pass! We have not been seen."

The man in white linen entered the earthen room, taking with him the aroma of strange perfumes. The peasant closed the door, and passed through the inner doorway into the yard, where the ass stood within the high walls, safe from being stolen. There the peasant, in great disquietude, tied up the cock. The man with the waxen face sat down on a mat near the hearth, for he was spent and barely conscious. Yet he heard outside the whispering of the peasant to his wife, for the woman had been watching from the roof.

Presently they came in, and the woman hid her face. She poured water, and put bread and dried figs on a wooden platter.

"Eat, Master!" said the peasant. "No one has seen."

But the stranger had no desire for food. Yet he moistened a little bread in the water, and ate it, since life must be. But desire was dead in him, even for food and drink. He had risen without desire, without even the desire to live, empty save for the all-overwhelming disillusion that lay like nausea where his life had been. Yet perhaps, deeper even than disillusion, was a desireless resoluteness, deeper even than consciousness.

12

The peasant and his wife stood near the door, watching. They saw with terror the livid wounds on the thin waxy hands and the thin feet of the stranger, and the small lacerations in the still dead forehead. They smelled with terror the scent of rich perfumes that came from him, from his body. And they looked at the fine, snowy, costly linen. Perhaps really he was a dead king, from the region of terrors. And he was still cold and remote in the region of death, with perfumes coming from his transparent body as if from some strange flower.

Having with difficulty swallowed some of the moistened bread, he lifted his eyes to them. He saw them as they were: limited, meagre in their life, without any splendour of gesture and of courage. But they were what they were, slow inevitable parts of the natural world. They had no nobility, but fear made them compassionate.

And the stranger had compassion on them again, for he knew that they would respond best to gentleness, giving back a clumsy gentleness again.

"Do not be afraid," he said to them gently. "Let me stay a little while with you. I shall not stay long. And then I shall go away forever. But do not be afraid. No harm will come to you through me."

They believed him at once, yet the fear did not leave them. And they said:

"Stay, Master, while ever you will. Rest! Rest quietly!"

But they were afraid.

So he let them be, and the peasant went away with the ass. The sun had risen bright, and in the dark house with the door shut, the man was again as if in the tomb. So he said to the woman, "I would lie in the yard."

And she swept the yard for him, and laid him a mat, and he lay down under the wall in the morning sun. There he saw the first green leaves spurting like flames from the ends of the enclosed fig-tree, out of the bareness to the sky of spring above. But the man who had died could not look, he only lay quite still in the sun, which was not yet too hot, and had no desire in him, not even to move. But he lay with his thin legs in the sun, his black perfumed hair falling into the hollows of his neck, and his thin colourless arms utterly inert. As he lay there, the hens clucked and scratched, and the escaped cock, caught and tied by the leg again, cowered in a corner.

The peasant woman was frightened. She came peeping, and, seeing him never move, feared to have a dead man in the yard. But the sun had grown stronger, he opened his eyes and looked at her. And now she was frightened of the man who was alive, but spoke nothing.

He opened his eyes, and saw the world again bright as glass. It was life, in which he had no share any more. But it shone outside him, blue sky, and a bare fig-tree with little jets of green leaf. Bright as glass, and he was not of it, for desire had failed.

Yet he was there, and not extinguished. The day passed in a kind of coma, and at evening he went into the house. The peasant man came home, but he was frightened, and had nothing to say. The stranger too ate of the mess of beans, a little. Then he washed his hands and turned to the wall, and was silent. The peasants were silent too. They watched their guest sleep. Sleep was so near death he could still sleep.

Yet when the sun came up, he went again to lie in the yard. The sun was the one thing that drew him and swayed him, and he still wanted to feel the cool air of morning in his nostrils, see the pale sky overhead. He still hated to be shut up.

As he came out, the young cock crowed. It was a diminished, pinched cry, but there was that in the voice of the bird stronger than chagrin. It was the necessity to live, and even to cry out the triumph of life. The man who had died stood and watched the cock who had escaped and been caught, ruffling himself up, rising forward on his toes, throwing up his head, and parting his beak in another challenge from life to death. The brave sounds rang out, and though they were diminished by the cord round the bird's leg, they were not cut off. The man who had died looked nakedly on life, and saw a vast resoluteness everywhere flinging itself up in stormy or subtle wave-crests, foam-tips emerging out of the blue invisible, a black and orange cock or the green flame-tongues out of the extremes of the fig-tree. They came forth, these things and creatures of spring, glowing with desire and with assertion. They came like crests of foam, out of the blue flood of the invisible desire, out of the vast invisible sea of strength, and they came coloured and tangible, evanescent, yet deathless in their coming. The man who had died looked on the great swing into existence of things that had not died, but he saw no longer their tremulous desire to exist and to be. He heard instead their ringing, ringing, defiant challenge to all other things existing.

The man lay still, with eyes that had died now wide open and darkly still, seeing the everlasting resoluteness of life. And the cock, with the flat, brilliant glance, glanced back at him with a bird's half-seeing look. And always the man who had died saw not the bird alone, but the short, sharp wave of life of which the bird was the crest. He watched the queer, beaky motion of the creature as it gobbled into itself the scraps of food; its glancing of the eye of life, ever alert and watchful, overweening and cautious, and the voice of its life, crowing triumph and assertion, yet strangled by a cord of circumstance. He seemed to hear the queer speech of very life, as the cock triumphantly imitated the clucking of the favourite hen, when she had laid an egg, a clucking which still had, in the male bird, the hollow chagrin of the cord round his leg. And when the man threw a bit of bread to the cock, it called with an extraordinary cooing tenderness, tousling and saving the morsel for the hens. The hens ran up greedily, and carried the morsel away beyond the reach of the string.

Then, walking complacently after them, suddenly the male bird's leg would hitch at the end of his tether, and he would yield with a kind of collapse. His flag fell, he seemed to diminish, he would huddle in the shade. And he was young, his tail-feathers, glossy as they were, were not fully grown. It was not till evening again that the tide of life in him made him forget. Then when his favourite hen came strolling unconcernedly near him, emitting the lure, he pounced on her with all his feathers vibrating. And the man who had died watched the unsteady, rocking vibration of the bent bird, and it was not the bird he saw, but one wave-tip of life overlapping for a minute another, in the tide of the swaying ocean of life. And the destiny of life seemed more fierce and compulsive to him even than the destiny of death. The doom of death was a shadow compared to the raging destiny of life, the determined surge of life.

At twilight the peasant came home with the ass, and he said: "Master! It is said that the body was stolen from the garden, and the tomb is empty, and the soldiers are taken away, accursed Romans! And the women are there to weep."

The man who had died looked at the man who had not died.

"It is well," he said. "Say nothing, and we are safe."

And the peasant was relieved. He looked rather dirty and stupid, and even as much flaminess as that of the young cock, which he had tied by the leg, would never glow in him. He was without fire. But the man who had died thought to himself: "Why, then, should he be lifted up? Clods of earth are turned over for refreshment, they are not to be lifted up. Let the earth remain earthy, and hold its own against the sky. I was wrong to seek to lift it up. I was wrong to try to interfere. The plough-share of devastation will be set in the soil of Judæa, and the life of this peasant will be overturned like the sods of the field. No man can save the earth from tillage. It is tillage, not salvation. . . ."

So he saw the man, the peasant, with compassion; but the man who had died no longer wished to interfere in the soul of the man who had not died, and who could never die, save to return to earth. Let him return to earth in his own good hour, and let no one try to interfere when the earth claims her own.

So the man with scars let the peasant go from him, for the peasant had no re-birth in him. Yet the man who had died said to himself: "He is my host."

And at dawn, when he was better, the man who had died rose up, and on slow, sore feet retraced his way to the garden. For he had been betrayed in a garden, and buried in a garden. And as he turned round the screen of laurels, near the rock-face, he saw a woman hovering by the tomb, a woman in blue and yellow. She peeped again into the mouth of the hole, that was like a deep cupboard. But still there was nothing. And she wrung her hands and wept. And as she turned away, she saw the man in white, standing by the laurels, and she gave a cry, thinking it might be a spy, and she said:

"They have taken him away!"

So he said to her:

"Madeleine!"

Then she reeled as if she would fall, for she knew him. And he said to her:

"Madeleine! Do not be afraid. I am alive. They took me down too soon, so I came back to life. Then I was sheltered in a house."

She did not know what to say, but fell at his feet to kiss them.

"Don't touch me, Madeleine," he said. "Not yet! I am not yet healed and in touch with men."

So she wept because she did not know what to do. And he said:

"Let us go aside, among the bushes, where we can speak unseen."

So in her blue mantle and her yellow robe, she followed him among the trees, and he sat down under a myrtle bush. And he said:

"I am not yet quite come to. Madeleine, what is to be done next?"

"Master!" she said. "Oh, we have wept for you! And will you come back to us?"

"What is finished is finished, and for me the end is past," he said.

"The stream will run till no more rains fill it, then it will dry up. For me, that life is over."

"And will you give up your triumph?" she said sadly.

"My triumph," he said, "is that I am not dead. I have outlived my mission, and know no more of it. It is my triumph. I have survived the day and the death of my interference, and am still a man. I am young still, Madeleine, not even come to middle age. I am glad all that is over. It had to be. But now I am glad it is over, and the day of my interference is done. The teacher and the saviour are dead in me; now I can go about my business, into my own single life."

She heard him, and did not fully understand. But what he said made her feel disappointed.

"But you will come back to us?" she said, insisting.

"I don't know what I shall do," he said. "When I am healed, I shall know better. But my mission is over, and my teaching is finished, and death has saved me from my own salvation. Oh, Madeleine, I want to take my single way in life, which is my portion. My public life is over, the life of my self-importance. Now I can wait on life, and say nothing, and have no one betray me. I wanted to be greater than the limits of my hands and feet, so I brought betrayal on myself. And I know I wronged Judas, my poor Judas. For I have died, and now I know my own limits. Now I can live without striving to sway others any more. For my reach ends in my finger-tips, and my stride is no longer than the ends of my toes. Yet I would embrace multitudes, I who have never truly embraced even one. But Judas and the high priests saved me from my own salvation, and soon I can turn to my destiny like a bather in the sea at dawn, who has just come down to the shore alone."

"Do you want to be alone henceforward?" she asked. "And was your mission nothing? Was it all untrue?"

"Nay!" he said. "Neither were your lovers in the past nothing. They were much to you, but you took more than you gave. Then you came to me for salvation from your own excess. And I, in my mission, I too ran to excess. I gave more than I took, and that also is woe and vanity. So Pilate and the high priests saved me from my own excessive salvation. Don't run to excess now in giving, Madeleine. It only means another death."

She pondered bitterly, for the need for excessive giving was in her, and she could not bear to be denied.

"And will you not come back to us?" she said. "Have you risen for yourself alone?"

He heard the sarcasm in her voice, and looked at her beautiful face which still was dense with excessive need for salvation from the woman she had been, the female who had caught men at her will. The cloud of necessity was on her, to be saved from the old, wilful Eve, who had embraced many men and taken more than she gave. Now the other doom was on her. She wanted to give without taking. And that, too, is hard, and cruel to the warm body.

"I have not risen from the dead in order to seek death again," he said.

She glanced up at him, and saw the weariness settling again on his waxy face, and the vast disillusion in his dark eyes, and the underlying indifference. He felt her glance, and said to himself:

24

"Now my own followers will want to do me to death again, for having risen up different from their expectation."

"But you will come to us, to see us, us who love you?" she said.

He laughed a little and said:

"Ah, yes." Then he added, "Have you a little money? Will you give me a little money? I owe it."

She had not much, but it pleased her to give it to him.

"Do you think," he said to her, "that I might come and live with you in your house?"

She looked up at him with large blue eyes, that gleamed strangely.

"Now?" she said, with peculiar triumph.

And he, who shrank now from triumph of any sort, his own or another's, said:

"Not now! Later, when I am healed, and ... and I am in touch with the flesh."

The words faltered in him. And in his heart he knew he would never go to live in her house. For the flicker of triumph had gleamed in her eyes; the greed of giving. But she murmured in a humming rapture:

"Ah, you know I would give up everything to you."

"Nay!" he said. "I didn't ask that."

A revulsion from all the life he had known came over him again, the great nausea of disillusion, and the spear-thrust through his bowels. He crouched under the myrtle bushes, without strength. Yet his eyes were open. And she looked at him again, and she saw that it was not the Messiah. The Messiah had not risen. The enthusiasm and the burning purity were gone, and the rapt youth. His youth was dead. This man was middle-aged and disillusioned, with a certain terrible indifference, and a resoluteness which love would never conquer. This was not the Master she had so adored, the young, flamy, unphysical exalter of her soul. This was nearer to the lovers she had known of old, but with a greater indifference to the personal issue, and a lesser susceptibility.

She was thrown out of the balance of her rapturous, anguished adoration. This risen man was the death of her dream.

"You should go now," he said to her. "Do not touch me, I am in death. I shall come again here, on the third day. Come if you will, at dawn. And we will speak again."

She went away, perturbed and shattered. Yet as she went, her mind discarded the bitterness of the reality, and she conjured up rapture and wonder, that the Master was risen and was not dead. He was risen, the Saviour, the exalter, the wonder-worker! He was risen, but not as man; as pure God, who should not be touched by flesh, and who should be rapt away into Heaven. It was the most glorious and most ghostly of the miracles.

Meanwhile the man who had died gathered himself together at last, and slowly made his way to the peasant's house. He was glad to go back to them, and away from Madeleine and his own associates. For the peasants had the inertia of earth and would let him rest, and as yet, would put no compulsion on him.

The woman was on the roof, looking for him. She was afraid that he had gone away. His presence in the house had become like gentle wine to her. She hastened to the door, to him.

26

"Where have you been?" she said. "Why did you go away?"

"I have been to walk in a garden, and I have seen a friend, who gave me a little money. It is for you."

He held out his thin hand, with the small amount of money, all that Madeleine could give him. The peasant's wife's eyes glistened, for money was scarce, and she said:

"Oh, Master! And is it truly mine?"

"Take it!" he said. "It buys bread, and bread brings life."

So he lay down in the yard again, sick with relief at being alone again. For with the peasants he could be alone, but his own friends would never let him be alone. And in the safety of the yard, the young cock was dear to him, as it shouted in the helpless zest of life, and finished in helpless humiliation of being tied by the leg. This day the ass stood swishing her tail under the shed. The man who had died lay down and turned utterly away from life, in the sickness of death in life.

But the woman brought wine and water, and sweetened cakes, and roused him, so that he ate a little, to please her. The day was hot, and as she crouched to serve him, he saw her breasts sway from her humble body, under her smock. He knew she wished he would desire her, and she was youngish, and not unpleasant. And he, who had never known a woman, would have desired her if he could. But he could not want her, though he felt gently towards her soft, crouching, humble body. But it was her thoughts, her consciousness, he could not mingle with. She was pleased with the money, and now she wanted to take more from him. She wanted the embrace of his body. But her little soul was hard, and

27

short-sighted, and grasping, her body had its little greed, and no gentle reverence of the return gift. So he spoke a quiet, pleasant word to her, and turned away. He could not touch the little, personal body, the little, personal life of this woman, nor in any other. He turned away from it without hesitation.

Risen from the dead, he had realised at last that the body, too, has its little life, and beyond that, the greater life. He was virgin, in recoil from the little, greedy life of the body. But now he knew that virginity is a form of greed; and that the body rises again to give and to take, to take and to give, ungreedily. Now he knew that he had risen for the woman, or women, who knew the greater life of the body, not greedy to give, not greedy to take, and with whom he could mingle his body. But having died, he was patient, knowing there was time, an eternity of time. And he was driven by no greedy desire, either to give himself to others, or to grasp anything for himself. For he had died.

The peasant came home from work, and said:

"Master, I thank you for the money. But we did not want it. And all I have is yours."

But the man who had died was sad, because the peasant stood there in the little, personal body, and his eyes were cunning and sparkling with the hope of greater rewards in money, later on. True, the peasant had taken him in free, and had risked getting no reward. But the hope was cunning in him. Yet even this was as men are made. So when the peasant would have helped him to rise, for night had fallen, the man who had died said:

28

"Don't touch me, brother. I am not yet risen to the Father."

The sun burned with greater splendour, and burnished the young cock brighter. But the peasant kept the string renewed, and the bird was a prisoner. Yet the flame of life burned up to a sharp point in the cock, so that it eyed askance and haughtily the man who had died. And the man smiled and held the bird dear, and he said to it:

"Surely thou art risen to the Father, among birds." And the young cock, answering, crowed.

When at dawn on the third morning the man went to the garden, he was absorbed, thinking of the greater life of the body, beyond the little, narrow, personal life. So he came through the thick screen of laurel and myrtle bushes, near the rock, suddenly, and he saw three women near the tomb. One was Madeleine, and one was the woman who had been his mother, and third was a woman he knew, called Joan. He looked up, and saw them all, and they saw him, and they were all afraid.

He stood arrested in the distance, knowing they were there to claim him back, bodily. But he would in no wise return to them. Pallid, in the shadow of a grey morning that was blowing to rain, he saw them, and turned away. But Madeleine hastened towards him.

"I did not bring them," she said. "They have come of themselves. See, I have brought you money! . . . Will you not speak to them?"

She offered him some gold pieces and he took them, saying:

"May I have this money? I shall need it. I cannot speak to them, for I am not yet ascended to the Father. And I must leave you now."

"Ah! Where will you go?" she cried.

He looked at her, and saw she was clutching for the man in him who had died and was dead, the man of his youth and his mission, of his chastity and his fear, of his little life, his giving without taking.

"I must go to my Father!" he said.

"And you will leave us? There is your mother!" she cried, turning round with the old anguish, which yet was sweet to her.

"But now I must ascend to my Father," he said, and he drew back into the bushes, and so turned quickly, and went away, saying to himself:

"Now I belong to no one and have no connection, and mission or gospel is gone from me. Lo! I cannot make even my own life, and what have I to save? . . . I can learn to be alone."

So he went back to the peasant's house, to the yard where the young cock was tied by the leg, with a string. And he wanted no one, for it was best to be alone; for the presence of people made him lonely. The sun and the subtle salve of spring healed his wounds, even the gaping wound of disillusion through his bowels was closing up. And his need of men and women, his fever to have them and to be saved by them, this too was healing in him. Whatever came of touch between himself and the race of men, henceforth, should come without trespass or compulsion. For he said to himself:

"I tried to compel them to live, so they compelled me to die. It is always so, with compulsion. The recoil kills the advance. Now is my time to be alone."

Therefore he went no more to the garden, but lay still and saw the sun, or walked at dusk across the olive slopes, among the green wheat, that rose a palm-breadth higher every sunny day. And always he thought to himself:

"How good it is to have fulfilled my mission, and to be beyond it. Now I can be alone, and leave all things to themselves, and the fig-tree may be barren if it will, and the rich may be rich. My way is my own alone."

So the green jets of leaves unspread on the fig-tree, with the bright, translucent, green blood of the tree. And the young cock grew brighter, more lustrous with the sun's burnishing; yet always tied by the leg with a string. And the sun went down more and more in pomp, out of the gold and red-flushed air. The man who had died was aware of it all, and he thought:

"The Word is but the midge that bites at evening. Man is tormented with words like midges, and they follow him right into the tomb. But beyond the tomb they cannot go. Now I have passed the place where words can bite no more and the air is clear, and there is nothing to say, and I am alone within my own skin, which is the walls of all my domain."

So he healed of his wounds, and enjoyed his immortality of being alive without fret. For in the tomb he had slipped that noose which we call care. For in the tomb he had left his striving self, which cares and asserts itself. Now his uncaring self healed and became whole within his skin, and he smiled to himself with pure aloneness, which is one sort of immortality.

Then he said to himself: "I will wander the earth, and say nothing.

For nothing is so marvellous as to be alone in the phenomenal world, which is raging, and yet apart. And I have not seen it, I was too much blinded by my confusion within it. Now I will wander among the stirring of the phenomenal world, for it is the stirring of all things among themselves which leaves me purely alone."

So he communed with himself, and decided to be a physician. Because the power was still in him to heal any man or child who touched his compassion. Therefore he cut his hair and his beard after the right fashion, and smiled to himself. And he bought himself shoes, and the right mantle, and put the right cloth over his head, hiding all the little scars. And the peasant said:

"Master, will you go forth from us?"

"Yes, for the time is come for me to return to men."

So he gave the peasant a piece of money, and said to him:

"Give me the cock that escaped and is now tied by the leg. For he shall go forth with me."

So for a piece of money the peasant gave the cock to the man who had died, and at dawn the man who had died set out into the phenomenal world, to be fulfilled in his own aloneness in the midst of it. For previously he had been too much mixed up in it. Then he had died. Now he must come back, to be alone in the midst. Yet even now he did not go quite alone, for under his arm, as he went, he carried the cock, whose tail fluttered gaily behind, and who craned his head excitedly, for he too was adventuring out for the first time into the wider phenomenal world, which is the stirring of the body of cocks also. And the peasant woman shed a few tears, but then went indoors, being a peasant, to look again at the pieces of money. And it seemed to her, a gleam came out of the pieces of money, wonderful.

The man who had died wandered on, and it was a sunny day. He looked around as he went, and stood aside as the pack-train passed by, towards the city. And he said to himself:

"Strange is the phenomenal world, dirty and clean together! And I am the same. Yet I am apart! And life bubbles variously. Why should I have wanted it to bubble all alike? What a pity I preached to them! A sermon is so much more likely to cake into mud, and to close the fountains, than is a psalm or a song. I made a mistake. I understand that they executed me for preaching to them. Yet they could not finally execute me, for now I am risen in my own aloneness, and inherit the earth, since I lay no claim on it. And I will be alone in the seethe of all things; first and foremost, forever, I shall be alone. But I must toss this bird into the seethe of phenomena, for he must ride his wave. How hot he is with life! Soon, in some place, I shall leave him among the hens. And perhaps one evening, I shall meet a woman who can lure my risen body, yet leave me my aloneness. For the body of my desire has died, and I am not in touch anywhere. Yet how do I know! All at least is life. And this cock gleams with bright aloneness, though he answers the lure of hens. And I shall hasten on to that village on the hill ahead of me; already I am tired and weak, and want to close my eyes to everything."

Hastening a little with the desire to have finished going, he overtook two men going slowly, and talking. And being soft-footed, he heard they were speaking of himself. And he remembered them, for he had known them in his life, the life of his mission. So he greeted them, but did not disclose himself in the dusk, and they did not know him. He said to them:

"What then of him who would be king, and was put to death for it?"

They answered suspiciously: "Why ask you of him?"

"I have known him, and thought much about him," he said.

So they replied: "He has risen."

"Yea! And where is he, and how does he live?"

"We know not, for it is not revealed. Yet he is risen, and in a little while will ascend unto the Father."

"Yea! And where then is his Father?"

"Know ye not? You are then of the Gentiles! The Father is in Heaven, above the cloud and the firmament."

"Truly? Then how will he ascend?"

"As Elijah the Prophet, he shall go up in a glory."

"Even into the sky."

"Into the sky."

"Then is he not risen in the flesh?"

"He is risen in the flesh."

"And will he take flesh up into the sky?"

"The Father in Heaven will take him up."

The man who had died said no more, for his say was over, and words beget words, even as gnats. But the man asked him: "Why do you carry a cock?"

"I am a healer," he said, "and the bird hath virtue."

"You are not a believer?"

"Yea! I believe the bird is full of life and virtue."

They walked on in silence after this, and he felt they disliked his answer. So he smiled to himself, for a dangerous phenomenon in the world is a man of narrow belief, who denies the right of his neighbour to be alone. And as they came to the outskirts of the village, the man who had died stood still in the gloaming and said in his old voice:

"Know ye me not?"

And they cried in fear: "Master!"

"Yea!" he said, laughing softly. And he turned suddenly away, down a side lane, and was gone under the wall before they knew.

So he came to an inn where the asses stood in the yard. And he called for fritters, and they were made for him. So he slept under a shed. But in the morning he was wakened by a loud crowing, and his cock's voice ringing in his ears. So he saw the rooster of the inn walking forth to battle, with his hens, a goodly number, behind him. Then the cock of the man who had died sprang forth, and a battle began between the birds. The man of the inn ran to save his rooster, but the man who had died said:

"If my bird wins I will give him thee. And if he lose, thou shalt eat him."

So the birds fought savagely, and the cock of the man who had died killed the common cock of the yard. Then the man who had died said to his young cock:

"Thou at least hast found thy kingdom, and the females to thy body. Thy aloneness can take on splendour, polished by the lure of thy hens."

And he left his bird there, and went on deeper into the phenomenal world, which is a vast complexity of entanglements and allurements. And he asked himself a last question:

"From what, and to what, could this infinite whirl be saved?"

So he went his way, and was alone. But the way of the world was past belief, as he saw the strange entanglement of passions and circumstance and compulsion everywhere, but always the dread insomnia of compulsion. It was fear, the ultimate fear of death, that made men mad. So always he must move on, for if he stayed, his neighbours wound the strangling of their fear and bullying round him. There was nothing he could touch, for all, in a mad assertion of the ego, wanted to put a compulsion on him, and violate his intrinsic solitude. It was the mania of cities and societies and hosts, to lay a compulsion upon a man, upon all men. For men and women alike were mad with the egoistic fear of their own nothingness. And he thought of his own mission, how he had tried to lay the compulsion of love on all men. And the old nausea came back on him. For there was no contact without a subtle attempt to inflict a compulsion. And already he had been compelled even into death. The nausea of the old wound broke out afresh, and he looked again on the world with repulsion, dreading its mean contacts.

PART TWO

The wind came cold and strong from inland, from the invisible snows of Lebanon. But the temple, facing south and west, towards Egypt, faced the splendid sun of winter as he curved down towards the sea, the warmth and radiance flooded in between the pillars of painted wood. But the sea was invisible, because of the trees, though its dashing sounded among the hum of pines. The air was turning golden to afternoon. The woman who served Isis stood in her yellow robe, and looked up at the steep slopes coming down to the sea, where the olive-trees silvered under the wind like water splashing. She was alone save for the goddess. And in the winter afternoon the light stood erect and magnificent off the invisible sea, filling the hills of the coast. She went towards the sun, through the grove of Mediterranean pine-trees and evergreen oaks, in the midst of which the temple stood, on a little, tree-covered tongue of land between two bays.

It was only a very little way, and then she stood among the dry trunks of the outermost pines, on the rocks under which the sea smote and sucked, facing the open where the bright sun gloried in winter. The sea was dark, almost indigo, running away from the land, and crested with white. The hand of the wind brushed it strangely with shadow, as it brushed the olives of the slopes with silver. And there was no boat out.

The three boats were drawn high up on the steep shingle of the little bay, by the small grey tower. Along the edge of the shingle ran a high wall, inside which was a garden occupying the brief flat of the bay, then rising in terraces up the steep slope of the coast. And there, some little way up, within another wall, stood the low white villa, white and alone as the coast, overlooking the sea. But higher, much higher up, where the olives had given way to pine-trees again, ran the coast road, keeping to the height to be above the gullies that came down to the bays.

Upon it all poured the royal sunshine of the January afternoon. Or rather, all was part of the great sun, glow and substance and immaculate loneliness of the sea, and pure brightness.

Crouching in the rocks above the dark water, which only swung up and down, two slaves, half naked, were dressing pigeons for the evening meal. They pierced the throat of a blue, live bird, and let the drops of blood fall into the heaving sea, with curious concentration. They were performing some sacrifice, or working some incantation. The woman of the temple, yellow and white and alone like a winter narcissus, stood between the pines of the small, humped peninsula where the temple secretly hid, and watched.

A black-and-white pigeon, vividly white, like a ghost escaped over the low dark sea, sped out, caught the wind, tilted, rode, soared and swept over the pine-trees, and wheeled away, a speck, inland. It had escaped. The priestess heard the cry of the boy slave, a garden slave of about seventeen. He raised his arms to heaven in anger as the pigeon wheeled away, naked and angry and young he held out his arms. Then he turned and seized the girl in an access of rage, and beat her with his

fist that was stained with pigeon's blood. And she lay down with her face hidden, passive and quivering. The woman who owned them watched. And as she watched, she saw another onlooker, a stranger, in a low, broad hat, and a cloak of grey homespun, a dark bearded man standing on the little causeway of a rock that was the neck of her temple peninsula. By the blowing of his dark-grey cloak she saw him. And he saw her, on the rocks like a white-and-yellow narcissus, because of the flutter of her white linen tunic, below the yellow mantle of wool. And both of them watched the two slaves.

The boy suddenly left off beating the girl. He crouched over her, touching her, trying to make her speak. But she lay quite inert, face down on the smoothed rock. And he put his arms round her and lifted her, but she slipped back to earth like one dead, yet far too quickly for anything dead. The boy, desperate, caught her by the hips and hugged her to him, turning her over there. There she seemed inert, all her fight was in her shoulders. He twisted her over, intent and unconscious, and pushed his hands between her thighs, to push them apart. And in an instant he was covering her in the blind, frightened frenzy of a boy's first passion. Quick and frenzied his young body quivered naked on hers, blind, for a minute. Then it lay quite still, as if dead.

And then, in terror, he peeped up. He peeped round, and drew slowly to his feet, adjusting his loin-rag. He saw the stranger, and then he saw, on the rocks beyond, the lady of Isis, his mistress. And as he saw her, his whole body shrank and cowed, and with a strange cringing motion he scuttled lamely towards the door in the wall.

The girl sat up and looked after him. When she had seen him disappear, she too looked round. And she saw the stranger and the priestess. Then with a sullen movement she turned away, as if she had seen nothing, to the four dead pigeons and the knife, which lay there on the rock. And she began to strip the small feathers, so that they rose on the wind like dust.

The priestess turned away. Slaves! Let the overseer watch them. She was not interested. She went slowly through the pines again, back to the temple, which stood in the sun in a small clearing at the centre of the tongue of land. It was a small temple of wood, painted all pink and white and blue, having at the front four wooden pillars rising like stems to the swollen lotus-bud of Egypt at the top, supporting the roof and open, spiky lotus-flowers of the outer frieze, which went round under the eaves. Two low steps of stone led up to the platform before the pillars, and the chamber behind the pillars was open. There a low stone altar stood, with a few embers in its hollow, and the dark stain of blood in its end groove.

She knew her temple so well, for she had built it at her own expense, and tended it for seven years. There it stood, pink and white, like a flower in the little clearing, backed by blackish evergreen oaks; and the shadow of afternoon was already washing over its pillar-bases.

She entered slowly, passing through to the dark inner chamber, lighted by a perfumed oil-flame. And once more she pushed shut the door, and once more she threw a few grains of incense on a brazier before the goddess, and once more she sat down before her goddess, in the almost-darkness, to muse, to go away into the dreams of the goddess.

It was Isis; but not Isis, Mother of Horus. It was Isis Bereaved, Isis in

46

Search. The goddess, in painted marble, lifted her face and strode, one thigh forward through the frail fluting of her robe, in the anguish of bereavement and of search. She was looking for the fragments of the dead Osiris, dead and scattered asunder, dead, torn apart, and thrown in fragments over the wide world. And she must find his hands and his feet, his heart, his thighs, his head, his belly, she must gather him together and fold her arms round the re-assembled body till it became warm again, and roused to life, and could embrace her, and could fecundate her womb. And the strange rapture and anguish of search went on through the years, as she lifted her throat and her hollowed eyes looked inward, in the tormented ecstasy of seeking, and the delicate navel of her bud-like belly showed through the frail, girdled robe with the eternal asking, asking, of her search. And through the years she found him bit by bit, heart and head and limbs and body. And yet she had not found the last reality, the final clue to him, that alone could bring him really back to her. For she was Isis of the subtle lotus, the womb which waits submerged and in bud, waits for the touch of that other inward sun that streams its rays from the loins of the male Osiris.

This was the mystery the woman had served alone for seven years, since she was twenty, till now she was twenty-seven. Before, when she was young, she had lived in the world, in Rome, in Ephesus, in Egypt. For her father had been one of Anthony's captains and comrades, had fought with Anthony and had stood with him when Cæsar was murdered, and through to the days of shame. Then he had come again across to Asia, out of favour with Rome, and had been killed in the mountains beyond Lebanon. The widow, having no favour to hope

47

for from Octavius, had retired to her small property on the coast under Lebanon, taking her daughter from the world, a girl of nineteen, beautiful but unmarried.

When she was young the girl had known Cæsar, and had shrunk from his eagle-like rapacity. The golden Anthony had sat with her many a half-hour, in the splendour of his great limbs and glowing manhood, and talked with her of the philosophies and the gods. For he was fascinated as a child by the gods, though he mocked at them, and forgot them in his own vanity. But he said to her:

"I have sacrificed two doves for you, to Venus, for I am afraid you make no offering to the sweet goddess. Beware you will offend her. Come, why is the flower of you so cool within? Does never a ray nor a glance find its way through? Ah, come, a maid should open to the sun, when the sun leans towards her to caress her."

And the big, bright eyes of Anthony laughed down on her, bathing her in his glow. And she felt the lovely glow of his male beauty and his amorousness bathe all her limbs and her body. But it was as he said: the very flower of her womb was cool, was almost cold, like a bud in shadow of frost, for all the flooding of his sunshine. So Anthony, respecting her father, who loved her, had left her.

And it had always been the same. She saw many men, young and old. And on the whole, she liked the old ones best, for they talked to her still and sincere, and did not expect her to open like a flower to the sun of their maleness. Once she asked a philosopher: "Are all women born to be given to men?" To which the old man answered slowly:

48

"Rare women wait for the re-born man. For the lotus, as you know, will not answer to all the bright heat of the sun. But she curves her dark, hidden head in the depths, and stirs not. Till, in the night, one of these rare, invisible suns that have been killed and shine no more, rises among the stars in unseen purple, and like the violet, sends its rare, purple rays out into the night. To these the lotus stirs as to a caress, and rises upwards through the flood, and lifts up her bent head, and opens with an expansion such as no other flower knows, and spreads her sharp rays of bliss, and offers her soft, gold depths such as no other flower possesses, to the penetration of the flooding, violet-dark sun that has died and risen and makes no show. But for the golden brief day-suns of show such as Anthony, and for the hard winter suns of power, such as Cæsar, the lotus stirs not, nor will ever stir. Those will only tear open the bud. Ah, I tell you, wait for the re-born and wait for the bud to stir."

So she had waited. For all the men were soldiers or politicians in the Roman spell, assertive, manly, splendid apparently, but of an inward meanness, an inadequacy. And Rome and Egypt alike had left her alone, unroused. And she was a woman to herself, she would not give herself for a surface glow, nor marry for reasons. She would wait for the lotus to stir.

And then, in Egypt, she had found Isis, in whom she spelled her mystery. She had brought Isis to the shores of Sidon, and lived with her in the mystery of search; whilst her mother, who loved affairs, controlled the small estate and the slaves with a free hand.

When the woman had roused from her muse and risen to perform the last brief ritual to Isis, she replenished the lamp and left the sanctuary, locking the door. In the outer world, the sun had already set, and twilight was chill among the humming trees, which hummed still, though the wind was abating.

A stranger in a dark broad hat rose from the corner of the temple steps, holding his hat in the wind. He was dark-faced, with a black pointed beard. "O Madam, whose shelter may I implore?" he said to the woman, who stood in her yellow mantle on a step above him, beside a pink-and-white painted pillar. Her face was rather long and pale, her dusky blond hair was held under a thin gold net. She looked down on the vagabond with indifference. It was the same she had seen watching the slaves.

"Why come you down from the road?" she asked.

"I saw the temple like a pale flower on the coast, and would rest among the trees of the precincts, if the lady of the goddess permits."

"It is Isis in Search," she said, answering his first question.

"The goddess is great," he replied.

She looked at him still with mistrust. There was a faint remote smile in the dark eyes lifted to her, though the face was hollow with suffering. The vagabond divined her hesitation, and was mocking her.

"Stay here upon the steps," she said. "A slave will show you the shelter."

"The lady of Egypt is gracious."

She went down the rocky path of the humped peninsula, in her gilded sandals. Beautiful were her ivory feet, beneath the white tunic, and above the saffron mantle her dusky-blond head bent as with endless musings. A woman entangled in her own dream. The man smiled a little, half-bitterly, and sat again on the step to wait, drawing his mantle round him, in the cold twilight.

At length a slave appeared, also in hodden grey.

"Seek ye the shelter of our lady?" he said insolently.

"Even so."

"Then come."

With the brusque insolence of a slave waiting on a vagabond, the young fellow led through the trees and down into a little gully in the rock, where, almost in darkness, was a small cave, with a litter of the tall heaths that grew on the waste places of the coast, under the stone-pines. The place was dark, but absolutely silent from the wind. There was still a faint odour of goats.

"Here sleep!" said the slave. "For the goats come no more on this half-island. And there is water!" He pointed to a little basin of rock where the maidenhair fern fringed a dripping mouthful of water.

Having scornfully bestowed his patronage, the slave departed. The man who had died climbed out to the tip of the peninsula, where the wave thrashed. It was rapidly getting dark, and the stars were coming out. The wind was abating for the night. Inland, the steep grooved upslope was dark to the long wavering outline of the crest against the translucent sky. Only now and then, a lantern flickered towards the villa.

The man who had died went back to the shelter. There he took bread from his leather pouch, dipped it in the water of the tiny spring, and slowly ate. Having eaten and washed his mouth, he looked once more at the bright stars in the pure windy sky, then settled the heath for his bed. Having laid his hat and his sandals aside, and put his pouch under his cheek for a pillow, he slept, for he was very tired. Yet during the night the cold woke him, pinching wearily through his weariness. Outside was brilliantly starry, and still windy. He sat and hugged himself in a sort of coma, and towards dawn went to sleep again.

In the morning the coast was still chill in shadow, though the sun was up behind the hills, when the woman came down from the villa towards the goddess. The sea was fair and pale blue, lovely in newness, and at last the wind was still. Yet the waves broke white in the many rocks, and tore in the shingle of the little bay. The woman came slowly, towards her dream. Yet she was aware of an interruption.

As she followed the little neck of rock on to her peninsula, and climbed the slope between the trees to the temple, a slave came down and stood, making his obeisance. There was a faint insolence in his humility.

"Speak!" she said.

"Lady, the man is there, he still sleeps. Lady, may I speak?"

"Speak!" she said, repelled by the fellow.

"Lady, the man is an escaped malefactor."

The slave seemed to triumph in imparting the unpleasant news.

"By what sign?"

"Behold his hands and feet! Will the lady look on him?"

"Lead on!"

The slave led quickly over the mound of the hill down to the tiny ravine. There he stood aside, and the woman went into the crack towards the cave. Her heart beat a little. Above all she must preserve her temple inviolate.

The vagabond was asleep with his cheek on his scrip, his mantle wrapped round him, but his bare, soiled feet curling side by side, to keep each other warm, and his hand lying loosely clenched in sleep. And in the pale skin of his feet, usually covered by sandalstraps, she saw the scars, and in the palm of the loose hand.

She had no interest in men, particularly in the servile class. Yet she looked at the sleeping face. It was worn, hollow, and rather ugly. But, a true priestess, she saw the other kind of beauty in it, the sheer stillness of the deeper life. There was even a sort of majesty in the dark brows, over the still, hollow cheeks. She saw that his black hair, left long, in contrast to the Roman fashion, was touched with grey at the temples, and the black pointed beard had threads of grey. But that must be suffering or misfortune, for the man was young. His dusky skin had the silvery glisten of youth still.

There was a beauty of much suffering, and the strange calm candour of finer life in the whole delicate ugliness of the face. For the first time, she was touched on the quick at the sight of a man, as if the tip of a fine flame of living had touched her. It was the first time. Men had roused all kinds of feeling in her, but never had touched her with the flame-tip of life.

She went back under the rock to where the slave waited.

"Know!" she said. "This is no malefactor, but a free citizen of the east. Do not disturb him. But when he comes forth, bring him to me; tell him I would speak with him."

She spoke coldly, for she found slaves invariably repellent, a little repulsive. They were so embedded in the lesser life, and their appetites and their small consciousness were a little disgusting. So she wrapped her dream round her, and went to the temple, where a slave-girl brought winter roses and jasmine, for the altar. But to-day, even in her ministrations, she was disturbed.

The sun rose over the hill, sparkling, the light fell triumphantly on the little pine-covered peninsula of the coast, and on the pink temple, in the pristine newness. The man who had died woke up, and put on his sandals. He put on his hat too, slung his scrip under his mantle, and went out, to see the morning in all its blue and its new gold. He glanced at the little yellow-and-white narcissus sparkling gaily in the rocks. And he saw the slave waiting for him like a menace.

"Master!" said the slave. "Our lady would speak with you at the house of Isis."

"It is well," said the wanderer.

He went slowly, staying to look at the pale blue sea like a flower in unruffled bloom, and the white fringes among the rocks, like white rock-flowers, the hollow slopes sheering up high from the shore, grey with olive-trees and green with bright young wheat, and set with the white small villa. All fair and pure in the January morning.

The sun fell on the corner of the temple, he sat down on the step in the sunshine, in the infinite patience of waiting. He had come back to life, but not the same life that he had left, the life of little people and the little day. Reborn, he was in the other life, the greater day of the human consciousness. And he was alone and apart from the little day, and out of contact with the daily people. Not yet had he accepted the irrevocable *noli me tangere* which separates the re-born from the vulgar. The separation was absolute, as yet here at the temple he felt peace, the hard, bright pagan peace with hostility of slaves beneath.

The woman came into the dark inner doorway of the temple, from the shrine, and stood there, hesitating. She could see the dark figure of the man, sitting in that terrible stillness that was portentous to her, had something almost menacing in its patience.

She advanced across the outer chamber of the temple, and the man, becoming aware of her, stood up. She addressed him in Greek, but he said:

"Madam, my Greek is limited. Allow me to speak vulgar Syrian."

"Whence come you? Whither go you?" she asked, with a hurried preoccupation of a priestess.

"From the east beyond Damascus—and I go west as the road goes," he replied slowly.

She glanced at him with sudden anxiety and shyness.

"But why do you have the marks of a malefactor?" she asked abruptly.

"Did the Lady of Isis spy upon me in my sleep?" he asked, with a grey weariness.

"The slave warned me—your hands and feet—" she said.

57

He looked at her. Then he said:

"Will the Lady of Isis allow me to bid her farewell, and go up to the road?"

The wind came in a sudden puff, lifting his mantle and his hat. He put his hand to hold the brim, and she saw again the thin brown hand with its scar.

"See! The scar!" she said, pointing.

"Even so!" he said. "But farewell, and to Isis my homage and my thanks for sleep."

He was going. But she looked up at him with her wondering blue eyes.

"Will you not look at Isis?" she said, with sudden impulse. And something stirred in him, like pain.

"Where then?" he said.

"Come!"

He followed her into the inner shrine, into the almost-darkness. When his eyes got used to the faint glow of the lamp, he saw the goddess striding like a ship, eager in the swirl of her gown, and he made his obeisance.

"Great is Isis!" he said. "In her search she is greater than death. Wonderful is such walking in a woman, wonderful the goal. All men praise thee, Isis, thou greater than the mother unto man."

The woman of Isis heard, and threw incense on the brazier. Then she looked at the man.

"Is it well with thee here?" she asked him. "Has Isis brought thee home to herself?"

He looked at the priestess in wonder and trouble.

"I know not," he said.

But the woman was pondering that this was the lost Osiris. She felt it in the quick of her soul. And her agitation was intense.

He would not stay in the close, dark, perfumed shrine. He went out again to the morning, to the cold air. He felt something approaching to touch him, and all his flesh was still woven with pain and the wild commandment: *Noli me tangere!* Touch me not! Oh, don't touch me!

The woman followed into the open with timid eagerness. He was moving away.

"Oh stranger, do not go! O stay awhile with Isis!"

He looked at her, at her face open like a flower, as if a sun had risen in her soul. And again his loins stirred.

"Would you detain me, girl of Isis?" he said.

"Stay! I am sure you are Osiris!" she said.

He laughed suddenly. "Not yet!" he said. Then he looked at her wistful face. "But I will sleep another night in the cave of the goats, if Isis wills it," he added.

She put her hands together with a priestess's childish happiness.

"Ah! Isis will be glad!" she said.

So he went down to the shore, in great trouble, saying to himself: "Shall I give myself into this touch? Shall I give myself into this touch? Men have tortured me to death with their touch. Yet this girl of Isis is a tender flame of healing. I am a physician, yet I have no healing like the flame of this tender girl. The flame of this tender girl! Like the first pale crocus of the spring. How could I have been blind to the healing and the bliss in the crocus-like body of a tender woman! Ah, tenderness! More terrible and lovely than the death I died—"

He pried small shell-fish from the rocks, and ate them with relish and wonder for the simple taste of the sea. And inwardly, he was tremulous, thinking: "Dare I come into touch? For this is further than death. I have dared to let them lay hands on me and put me to death. But dare I come into this tender touch of life? Oh, this is harder—"

But the woman went into the shrine again, and sat rapt in pure muse, through the long hours, watching the swirling stride of the yearning goddess, and the navel of the bud-like belly, like a seal on the virgin urge of the search. And she gave herself to the woman-flow and to the urge of Isis in Search.

Towards sundown she went on the peninsula to look for him. And she found him gone towards the sun, as she had gone the day before, and sitting on the pine-needles at the foot of the tree, where she had stood when first she saw him. Now she approached tremulously and slowly, afraid lest he did not want her. She stood near him unseen, till suddenly he glanced up at her from under his broad hat, and saw the westering sun on her netted hair. He was startled, yet he expected her.

"Is that your home?" he said, pointing to the white low villa on the slope of olives.

"It is my mother's house. She is a widow, and I am her only child."

"And are these all her slaves?"

"Except those that are mine."

Their eyes met for a moment.

"Will you too sit to see the sun go down?" he said.

He had not risen to speak to her. He had known too much pain. So she sat on the dry brown pine-needles, gathering her saffron mantle round her knees. A boat was coming in, out of the open glow into the shadow of the bay, and slaves were lifting small nets, their babble coming off the surface of the water.

"And this is home to you," he said.

"But I serve Isis in Search," she replied.

He looked at her. She was like a soft, musing cloud, somehow remote. His soul smote him with passion and compassion.

"Mayst thou find thy desire, maiden," he said, with sudden earnestness.

"And art thou not Osiris?" she asked.

He flushed suddenly.

"Yes, if thou wilt heal me!" he said. "For the death aloofness is still upon me, and I cannot escape it."

She looked at him for a moment in fear, from the soft blue sun of her eyes. Then she lowered her head, and they sat in silence in the warmth and glow of the western sun: the man who had died, and the woman of the pure search.

The sun was curving down to the sea, in grand winter splendour. It fell on the twinkling, naked bodies of the slaves, with their ruddy broad hams and their small black heads, as they ran spreading the nets on the pebble beach. The all-tolerant Pan watched over them. All-tolerant Pan should be their god forever.

The woman rose as the sun's rim dipped, saying:

"If you will stay, I shall send down victual and covering."

63

"The lady your mother, what will she say?"

The woman of Isis looked at him strangely, but with a tinge of misgiving.

"It is my own," she said.

"It is good," he said, smiling faintly, and foreseeing difficulties.

He watched her go, with her absorbed, strange motion of the self-dedicate. Her dun head was a little bent, the white linen swung about her ivory ankles. And he saw the naked slaves stand to look at her, with a certain wonder, and even a certain mischief. But she passed intent through the door in the wall, on the bay.

The man who had died sat on at the foot of the tree overlooking the strand, for on the little shore everything happened. At the small stream which ran in round the corner of the property wall, women slaves were still washing linen, and now and again came the hollow chock! chock! chock! as they beat it against the smooth stones, in the dark little hollow of the pool. There was a smell of olive-refuse on the air; and sometimes still the faint rumble of the grindstone that was milling the olives, inside the garden, and the sound of the slave calling to the ass at the mill. Then through the doorway a woman stepped, a grey-haired woman in a mantle of whitish wool, and there followed her a bare-headed man in a toga, a Roman: probably her steward or overseer. They stood on the high shingle above the sea, and cast round a rapid glance. The broad-hammed, ruddy-bodied slaves bent absorbed and abject over the nets, picking them clean, the women washing linen thrust their palms with energy down on the wash, the old slave bent absorbed at the water's edge, washing the fish and the polyps of the catch. And the woman and the overseer saw it all, in one glance. They also saw, seated at the foot of the tree on the rocks of the peninsula, the strange man silent and alone. And the man who had died saw that they spoke of him. Out of the little sacred world of the peninsula he looked on the common world, and saw it still hostile.

The sun was touching the sea, across the tiny bay stretched the shadow of the opposite humped headland. Over the shingle, now blue and cold in shadow, the elderly woman trod heavily, in shadow too, to look at the fish spread in the flat basket of the old man crouching at the water's edge: a naked old slave with fat hips and shoulders, on whose soft, fairish-orange body the last sun twinkled, then died. The old slave continued cleaning the fish absorbedly, not looking up: as if the lady were the shadow of twilight falling on him.

Then from the gateway stepped two slave-girls with flat baskets on their heads, and from one basket the terra-cotta wine-jar and the oil-jar poked up, leaning slightly. Over the massive shingle, under the wall, came the girls, and the woman of Isis in her saffron mantle stepped in twilight after them. Out at sea, the sun still shone. Here was shadow. The mother with grey head stood at the sea's edge and watched the daughter, all yellow and white, with dun blond head, swinging unseeing and unheeding after the slave-girls, towards the neck of rock of the peninsula; the daughter, travelling in her absorbed other-world. And not moving from her place, the elderly mother watched that procession of three file up the rise of the headland, between the trees, and disappear, shut in by trees. No slave had lifted a head to look. The grey-haired woman still watched the trees where her daughter had disappeared.

Then she glanced again at the foot of the tree, where the man who had died was still sitting, inconspicuous now, for the sun had left him; and only the far blade of the sea shone bright. It was evening. Patience! Let destiny move!

The mother plodded with a stamping stride up the shingle: not long and swinging and rapt, like the daughter, but short and determined. Then down the rocks opposite came two naked slaves trotting with huge bundles of dark green on their shoulders, so their broad, naked legs twinkled underneath like insects' legs, and their heads were hidden. They came trotting across the shingle, heedless and intent on their way, when suddenly the man, the Roman-looking overseer, addressed them, and they stopped dead. They stood invisible under their loads, as if they might disappear altogether, now they were arrested. Then a hand came out and pointed to the peninsula. Then the two green-heaped slaves trotted on, towards the temple precincts. The grey-haired woman joined the man, and slowly the two passed through the door again, from the shingle of the sea to the property of the villa. Then the old, fat-shouldered slave rose, pallid in the shadow, with his tray of fish from the sea, and the women rose from the pool, dusky and alive, piling the wet linen in a heap on to the flat baskets, and the slaves who had cleaned the net gathered its whitish folds together. And the old slave with the fish basket on his shoulder, and the women slaves with the heaped baskets of wet linen on their heads, and the two slaves with the folded net, and the slave with oars on his shoulders, and the boy with the folded sail on his arm, gathered in a naked group near the door, and the man

who had died heard the low buzz of their chatter. Then as the wind wafted cold, they began to pass through the door.

It was the life of the little day, the life of little people. And the man who had died said to himself: "Unless we encompass it in the greater day, and set the little life in the circle of the greater life, all is disaster."

Even the tops of the hills were in shadow. Only the sky was still upwardly radiant. The sea was a vast milky shadow. The man who had died rose a little stiffly, and turned into the grove.

There was no one at the temple. He went on to his lair in the rock. There, the slave-men had carried out the old heath of the bedding, swept the rock floor, and were spreading with nice art the myrtle, then the rougher heath, then the soft, bushy heath-tips on top, for a bed. Over it all they put a well-tanned white ox-skin. The maids had laid folded woollen covers at the head of the cave, and the wine-jar, the oil-jar, a terra-cotta drinking-cup, and a basket containing bread, salt, cheese, dried figs and eggs stood neatly arranged. There was also a little brazier of charcoal. The cave was suddenly full, and a dwelling-place.

The woman of Isis stood in the hollow by the tiny spring.

Only one slave at a time could pass. The girl-slaves waited at the entrance to the narrow place. When the man who had died appeared, the woman sent the girls away. The men-slaves still arranged the bed, making the job as long as possible. But the woman of Isis dismissed them too. And the man who had died came to look at his house.

"Is it well?" the woman asked him.

"It is very well," the man replied. "But the lady, your mother, and he who is no doubt the steward, watched while the slaves brought the goods. Will they not oppose you?"

"I have my own portion! Can I not give of my own? Who is going to oppose me and the gods?" she said, with a certain soft fury, touched with exasperation. So that he knew that her mother would oppose her, and that the spirit of the little life would fight against the spirit of the greater. And he thought: "Why did the woman of Isis relinquish her portion in the daily world? She should have kept her goods fiercely!"

"Will you eat and drink?" she said. "On the ashes are warm eggs. And I will go up to the meal at the villa. But in the second hour of the night I shall come down to the temple. O, then, will you come too to Isis?" She looked at him, and a queer glow dilated her eyes. This was her dream, and it was greater than herself. He could not bear to thwart her or hurt her in the least thing now. She was in the full glow of her woman's mystery.

"Shall I wait at the temple?" he said.

"O, wait at the second hour and I shall come." He heard the humming supplication in her voice and his fibres quivered.

"But the lady, your mother?" he said gently.

The woman looked at him, startled.

"She will not thwart me!" she said.

So he knew that the mother would thwart the daughter, for the daughter had left her goods in the hands of her mother, who would hold fast to this power.

But she went, and the man who had died lay reclining on his couch,

70

and ate the eggs from the ashes, and dipped his bread in oil, and ate it, for his flesh was dry: and he mixed wine and water, and drank. And so he lay still, and the lamp made a small bud of light.

He was absorbed and enmeshed in new sensations. The woman of Isis was lovely to him, not so much in form, as in the wonderful womanly glow of her. Suns beyond suns had dipped her in mysterious fire, the mysterious fire of a potent woman, and to touch her was like touching the sun. Best of all was her tender desire for him, like sunshine, so soft and still.

"She is like sunshine upon me," he said to himself, stretching his limbs. "I have never before stretched my limbs in such sunshine as her desire for me. The greatest of all gods granted me this."

At the same time he was haunted by the fear of the outer world. "If they can, they will kill us," he said to himself. "But there is a law of the sun which protects us."

And again he said to himself: "I have risen naked and branded. But if I am naked enough for this contact, I have not died in vain. Before I was clogged."

He rose and went out. The night was chill and starry, and of a great wintery splendour. "There are destinies of splendour," he said to the night, "after all our doom of littleness and meanness and pain."

So he went up silently to the temple, and waited in darkness against the inner wall, looking out on a grey darkness, stars, and rims of trees. And he said again to himself: "There are destinies of splendour, and there is a greater power."

So at last he saw the light of her silk lanthorn swinging, coming intermittent between the trees, yet coming swiftly. She was alone, and near, the light softly swishing on her mantle-hem. And he trembled with fear and with joy, saying to himself: "I am almost more afraid of this touch than I was of death. For I am more nakedly exposed to it."

"I am here, Lady of Isis," he said softly out of the dark.

"Ah!" she cried, in fear also, yet in rapture. For she was given to her dream.

She unlocked the door of the shrine, and he followed after her. Then she latched the door shut again. The air inside was warm and close and perfumed. The man who had died stood by the closed door, and watched the woman. She had come first to the goddess. And dim-lit, the goddess-statue stood surging forward, a little fearsome like a great woman-presence urging.

The priestess did not look at him. She took off her saffron mantle and laid it on a low couch. In the dim light she was bare armed, in her girdled white tunic. But she was still hiding herself away from him. He stood back in shadow, and watched her slowly fan the brazier and fling on incense. Faint clouds of sweet aroma arose on the air. She turned to the statue in the ritual of approach, softly swaying forward with a slight lurch, like a moored boat, tipping towards the goddess.

He watched the strange rapt woman, and he said to himself: "I must leave her alone in her rapture, her female mysteries." So she tipped in her strange forward-swaying rhythm before the goddess. Then she broke into a murmur of Greek, which he could not understand. And, as she murmured, her swaying softly subsided, like a boat on a sea that grows still. And as he watched her, he saw her soul in its aloneness, and its female difference. He said to himself: "How different she is from me, how strangely different! She is afraid of me, and my male difference. She is getting herself naked and clear of her fear. How sensitive and softly alive she is, with a life so different from mine! How beautiful with a soft strange courage, of life, so different from my courage of death! What a beautiful thing, like the heart of a rose, like the core of a flame. She is making herself completely penetrable. Ah! how terrible to fail her, or to trespass on her!"

She turned to him, her face glowing from the goddess.

"You are Osiris, aren't you?" she said naïvely.

"If you will," he said.

"Will you let Isis discover you? Will you not take off your things?"

He looked at the woman, and lost his breath. And his wounds, and especially the death-wound through his belly, began to cry again.

"It has hurt so much!" he said. "You must forgive me if I am still held back."

But he took off his cloak and his tunic, and went naked towards the idol, his breast panting with the sudden terror of overwhelming pain, memory of overwhelming pain, and grief too bitter.

"They did me to death!" he said in excuse of himself, turning his face to her for a moment.

And she saw the ghost of the death in him, as he stood there thin and stark before her, and suddenly she was terrified, and she felt robbed. She felt the shadow of the grey, grisly wing of death triumphant.

"Ah, Goddess," he said to the idol, in the vernacular. "I would be so glad to live, if you would give me my clue again."

For here again he felt desperate, faced by the demand of life, and burdened still by his death.

"Let me anoint you!" the woman said to him softly. "Let me anoint the scars! Show me, and let me anoint them!"

He forgot his nakedness in this re-evoked old pain. He sat on the edge of the couch, and she poured a little ointment into the palm of his hand. And as she chafed his hand, it all came back, the nails, the holes, the cruelty, the unjust cruelty against him who had offered only kindness. The agony of injustice and cruelty came over him again, as in his death-hour. But she chafed the palm, murmuring: "What was torn becomes a new flesh, what was a wound is full of fresh life; this scar is the eye of the violet."

And he could not help smiling at her, in her naïve priestess's absorption. This was her dream, and he was only a dream-object to her. She would never know or understand what he was. Especially she would never know the death that was gone before in him. But what did it matter? She was different. She was woman: her life and her death were different from his. Only she was good to him.

When she chafed his feet with oil and tender, tender healing, he could not refrain from saying to her:

"Once a woman washed my feet with tears, and wiped them with her hair, and poured on precious ointment."

The woman of Isis looked up at him from her earnest work, interrupted again.

"Were they hurt then?" she said. "Your feet?"

"No, no! It was while they were whole."

"And did you love her?"

"Love had passed in her. She only wanted to serve," he replied. "She had been a prostitute."

"And did you let her serve you?" she asked.

"Yea."

"Did you let her serve you with the corpse of her love?"

"Ay!"

Suddenly it dawned on him: "I asked them all to serve me with the corpse of their love. And in the end I offered them only the corpse of my love. This is my body—take and eat—my corpse—"

A vivid shame went through him. "After all," he thought, "I wanted them to love with dead bodies. If I had kissed Judas with live love, perhaps he would never have kissed me with death. Perhaps he loved me in the flesh, and I willed that he should love me bodylessly, with the corpse of love—"

There dawned on him the reality of the soft warm love which is in touch, and which is full of delight. "And I told them, blessed are they that mourn," he said to himself. "Alas, if I mourned even this woman here, now I am in death, I should have to remain dead, and I want so much to live. Life has brought me to this woman with warm hands. And her touch is more to me now than all my words. For I want to live—"

"Go then to the goddess!" she said softly, gently pushing him towards Isis. And as he stood there dazed and naked as an unborn thing, he heard the woman murmuring to the goddess, murmuring, murmuring with a plaintive appeal. She was stooping now, looking at the scar in the soft flesh of the socket of his side, a scar deep and like an eye sore

75

with endless weeping, just in the soft socket above the hip. It was here that his blood had left him, and his essential seed. The woman was trembling softly and murmuring in Greek. And he in the recurring dismay of having died, and in the anguished perplexity of having tried to force life, felt his wounds crying aloud, and the deep places of the body howling again: "I have been murdered, and I lent myself to murder. They murdered me, but I lent myself to murder—"

The woman, silent now, but quivering, laid oil in her hand and put her palm over the wound in his right side. He winced, and the wound absorbed his life again, as thousands of times before. And in the dark, wild pain and panic of his consciousness rang only one cry: "Oh, how can she take this death out of me? How can she take from me this death? She can never know! She can never understand! She can never equal it! . . ."

In silence, she softly rhythmically chafed the scar with oil. Absorbed now in her priestess's task, softly, softly gathering power, while the vitals of the man howled in panic. But as she gradually gathered power, and passed in a girdle round him to the opposite scar, gradually warmth began to take the place of the cold terror, and he felt: "I am going to be warm again, and I am going to be whole! I shall be warm like the morning. I shall be a man. It doesn't need understanding. It needs newness. She brings me newness—"

And he listened to the faint, ceaseless wail of distress of his wounds, sounding as if forever under the horizons of his consciousness. But the wail was growing dim, more dim.

He thought of the woman toiling over him: "She does not know!

She does not realise the death in me. But she has another consciousness. She comes to me from the opposite end of the night."

Having chafed all his lower body with oil, having worked with her slow intensity of a priestess, so that the sound of his wounds grew dimmer and dimmer, suddenly she put her breast against the wound in his left side, and her arms round him, folding over the wound in his right side, and she pressed him to her, in a power of living warmth, like the folds of a river. And the wailing died out altogether, and there was a stillness, and darkness in his soul, unbroken dark stillness, wholeness.

Then slowly, slowly, in the perfect darkness of his inner man, he felt the stir of something coming. A dawn, a new sun. A new sun was coming up in him, in the perfect inner darkness of himself. He waited for it breathless, quivering with a fearful hope ... "Now I am not myself. I am something new ..."

And as it rose, he felt, with a cold breath of disappointment, the girdle of the living woman slip down from him, the warmth and the glow slipped from him, leaving him stark. She crouched, spent, at the feet of the goddess, hiding her face.

Stooping, he laid his hand softly on her warm, bright shoulder, and the shock of desire went through him, shock after shock, so that he wondered if it were another sort of death: but full of magnificence.

Now all his consciousness was there in the crouching, hidden woman. He stooped beside her and caressed her softly, blindly, murmuring inarticulate things. And his death and his passion of sacrifice were all as nothing to him now, he knew only the crouching fulness of the woman there, the soft white rock of life. . . . "On this rock I built my life." The deep-folded, penetrable rock of the living woman! The woman, hiding her face. Himself bending over, powerful and new like dawn.

He crouched to her, and he felt the blaze of his manhood and his power rise up in his loins, magnificent.

"I am risen!"

Magnificent, blazing indomitable in the depths of his loins, his own sun dawned, and sent its fire running along his limbs, so that his face shone unconsciously.

He untied the string on the linen tunic, and slipped the garment down, till he saw the white glow of her white-gold breasts. And he touched them, and he felt his life go molten. "Father!" he said, "why did you hide this from me?" And he touched her with the poignancy of wonder, and the marvellous piercing transcendence of desire. "Lo!" he said, "this is beyond prayer." It was the deep, interfolded warmth, warmth living and penetrable, the woman, the heart of the rose! "My mansion is the intricate warm rose, my joy is this blossom!"

She looked up at him suddenly, her face like a lifted light, wistful, tender, her eyes like many wet flowers. And he drew her to his breast with a passion of tenderness and consuming desire, and the last thought: "My hour is upon me, I am taken unawares—"

So he knew her, and was one with her.

Afterwards, with a dim wonder, she touched the great scars in his sides with her finger-tips, and said:

"But they no longer hurt?"

"They are suns!" he said. "They shine from your touch. They are my atonement with you."

And when they left the temple, it was the coldness before dawn. As he closed the door, he looked again at the goddess, and he said: "Lo, Isis is a kindly goddess; and full of tenderness. Great gods are warm-hearted, and have tender goddesses."

The woman wrapped herself in her mantle and went home in silence, sightless, brooding like the lotus softly shutting again, with its god core full of fresh life. She saw nothing, for her own petals were a sheath to her. Only she thought: "I am full of Osiris. I am full of the risen Osiris! . . ."

But the man looked at the vivid stars before dawn, as they rained down to the sea, and the dog-star green towards the sea's rim. And he thought: "How plastic it is, how full of curves and folds like an invisible rose of dark-petalled openness that shows where the dew touches its darkness! How full it is, and great beyond all gods. How it leans around me, and I am part of it, the great rose of Space. I am like a grain of its perfume, and the woman is a grain of its beauty. Now the world is one flower of many petalled darknesses, and I am in its perfume as in a touch."

So, in the absolute stillness and fulness of touch, he slept in his cave while the dawn came. And after the dawn, the wind rose and brought a storm, with cold rain. So he stayed in his cave in the peace and the delight of being in touch, delighting to hear the sea, and the rain on the earth, and to see one white-and-gold narcissus bowing wet, and still wet. And he said: "This is the great atonement, the being in touch. The grey sea and the rain, the wet narcissus and the woman I wait for, the invisible Isis and the unseen sun are all in touch, and at one."

He waited at the temple for the woman, and she came in the rain. But she said to him:

"Let me sit awhile with Isis. And come to me, will you come to me, in the second hour of night?"

So he went back to the cave and lay in stillness and in the joy of being in touch, waiting for the woman who would come with the night, and consummate again the contact. Then when night came the woman came, and came gladly, for her great yearning too was upon her, to be in touch, to be in touch with him, nearer.

So the days came, and the nights came, and days came again, and the contact was perfected and fulfilled. And he said: "I will ask her nothing, not even her name, for a name would set her apart."

And she said to herself: "He is Osiris. I wish to know no more."

Plum-blossom blew from the trees, the time of the narcissus was past, anemones lit up the ground and were gone, the perfume of bean-field was in the air. All changed, the blossom of the universe changed its petals and swung round to look another way. The spring was fulfilled, a contact was established, the man and the woman were fulfilled of one another, and departure was in the air.

One day he met her under the trees, when the morning sun was hot, and the pines smelled sweet, and on the hills the last pear-bloom was scattering. She came slowly towards him, and in her gentle lingering, her tender hanging back from him, he knew a change in her.

"Hast thou conceived?" he asked her.

"Why?" she said.

"Thou art like a tree whose green leaves follow the blossom, full of sap. And there is a withdrawing about thee."

"It is so," she said. "I am with young by thee. Is it good?"

"Yea!" he said. "How should it not be good? So the nightingale calls no more from the valley-bed. But where wilt thou bear the child, for I am naked of all but life."

"We will stay here," she said.

"But the lady, your mother?"

A shadow crossed her brow. She did not answer.

"What when she knows?" he said.

"She begins to know."

"And would she hurt you?"

"Ah, not me! What I have is all my own. And I shall be big with Osiris. . . . But thou, do you watch her slaves."

She looked at him, and the peace of her maternity was troubled by anxiety.

"Let not your heart be troubled!" he said. "I have died the death once."

So he knew the time was come again for him to depart. He would go alone, with his destiny. Yet not alone, for the touch would be upon him, even as he left his touch on her. And invisible suns would go with him.

Yet he must go. For here on the bay the little life of jealousy and property was resuming sway again, as the suns of passionate fecundity relaxed their sway. In the name of property, the widow and her slaves would seek to be revenged on him for the bread he had eaten, and the living touch he had established, the woman he had delighted in. But he said: "Not twice! They shall not now profane the touch in me. My wits against theirs."

83

So he watched. And he knew they plotted. So he moved from the little cave, and found another shelter, a tiny cove of sand by the sea, dry and secret under the rocks.

He said to the woman:

"I must go now soon. Trouble is coming to me from the slaves. But I am a man, and the world is open. But what is between us is good, and is established. Be at peace. And when the nightingale calls again from your valley-bed, I shall come again, sure as Spring."

She said: "O don't go! Stay with me on half the island, and I will build a house for you and me under the pine-trees by the temple, where we can live apart."

Yet she knew that he would go. And even she wanted the coolness of her own air around her, and the release from anxiety.

"If I stay," he said, "they will betray me to the Romans and to their justice. But I will never be betrayed again. So when I am gone, live in peace with the growing child. And I shall come again; all is good between us, near or apart. The suns come back in their seasons: and I shall come again."

"Do not go yet," she said. "I have set a slave to watch at the neck of the peninsula. Do not go yet, till the harm shows."

But as he lay in his little cove, on a calm, still night, he heard the soft knock of oars, and the bump of a boat against the rock. So he crept out to listen. And he heard the Roman overseer say:

"Lead softly to the goat's den. And Lysippus shall throw the net over the malefactor while he sleeps, and we will bring him before justice, and the Lady of Isis shall know nothing of it . . ."

84

The man who had died caught a whiff of flesh from the oiled and naked slaves as they crept up, then the faint perfume of the Roman. He crept nearer to the sea. The slave who sat in the boat sat motionless, holding the oars, for the sea was quite still. And the man who had died knew him.

So out of the deep cleft of a rock he said, in a clear voice:

"Art thou not that slave who possessed the maiden under the eyes of Isis? Art thou not the youth? Speak!"

The youth stood up in the boat in terror. His movement sent the boat bumping against the rock. The slave sprang out in wild fear, and fled up the rocks. The man who had died quickly seized the boat and stepped in, and pushed off. The oars were yet warm with the unpleasant warmth of the hands of the slaves. But the man pulled slowly out, to get into the current which set down the coast, and would carry him in silence. The high coast was utterly dark against the starry night. There was no glimmer from the peninsula: the priestess came no more at night. The man who had died rowed slowly on, with the current, and laughed to himself: "I have sowed the seed of my life and my resurrection, and put my touch forever upon the choice woman of this day, and I carry her perfume in my flesh like essence of roses. She is dear to me in the middle of my being. But the gold and flowing serpent is coiling up again, to sleep at the root of my tree.

"So let the boat carry me. To-morrow is another day."

COMMENTARY ON
THE MAN WHO
DIED

I TOLD A NUMBER OF PEOPLE, some academic, that I was hoping to write a commentary for this edition; and alas, met a mixture of cynicism and commiseration, if not very plain distaste. Lawrence was third (just beaten by Dostoyevsky and George Eliot, if I remember) on H.L. Mencken's list of the ten most boring writers of all time. F.R. Leavis's fine study of Lawrence in 1955 showed that the other Eliot, Thomas Stearns, was archiepiscopally — and very unpoetically — dismissive of him. Sadly few of those, especially among the non-academics I spoke to, seemed anxious to treat him much more kindly. Lawrence, or at any rate that last-period Lawrence, was clearly no longer with it, quite *passé*. Death had sunk him out of sight like a deep-diving whale and therefore, in this ever less tolerant (and literate) world, out of mind. This is a common fate with the much studied, of course, one of those "snatches of lovely oblivion and snatches of renewal" on "the longest journey" — that wouldn't have distressed Lawrence or his once living self. I can't imagine he ever seriously doubted that in *human* memory he would stay as fixed as a star in heaven — or a species of flower on earth. He needed no wreaths, and knew his little ship of death would sail through all the doubts, decryings, and disparagements. As indeed, in all practical terms, it has; yet he had always (he loved paradox, falling in hate as well as in love) risked rough seas for his human name, if not his non-human soul.

Above all this isn't the age for sermons. We can tolerate smart slogans, good advertising copy, fluent jargon ... but Lawrence sometimes seems impossible. Anyone would think the man hadn't read a single word on deconstruction, or postmodern theory, or political correctness ... a dozen other vitally important matters. To say what you mean is hard enough; to sound as if you actually mean what you say is preposterous: ludicrously naive.

Born in 1926, four years before Lawrence himself died, I still hold some no doubt disgracefully antediluvian (to anyone smarter and younger) views both on literary and other values. Words (and how they're used) continue to fascinate and haunt me.

I still, dullard that I am, can't accept that since they all equally deal with signs, his poems (or Blake's, Shelley's, anyone else's) must be classed with the dullest commercial or the most abstruse scientific texts. In short I can't discount Lawrence as seems nowadays increasingly expected of his readers. He remains to me of the dimensions, in the context of both the Victorian and our own times, of a peak in the Everest range, or of the importance of rich old cities like Rome or Paris, or of the value of some whole botanical genus, an oak or primrose family — much too lastingly significant to be forgotten. Lawrence is very big; you may criticize and despise him, but you had better do it bigly also. Neither sniggers nor a latter-day Pecksniffianism are enough.

I am an atheist (more of that later) as to all ideas of an established and intervenient God; but not in my belief that there are comparative worths, in science as in the arts and affecting us both as members of society and as individuals. Some objects and ideas *do* have value, though others may be as futile as a film star's fart — and only too often, as noisome. Above all I loathe the drift (a kind of fascism of the majority) that would so homogenize, suburbanize, and "democratize" life that it loses all its varieties and roughnesses — that would make it, like margarine, "easy to spread." If we attempt to destroy all distinctions — and especially those (for example in education, sensitivity, intelligence, and passion) to which we can personally lay no great claim, perhaps other people won't notice that we're actually rather dull and ordinary or that (horror of horrors) there are others who are different.

> *There are too many people on earth*
> *insipid, unsalted, rabbity, endlessly hopping.*
> *They nibble the face of the earth to a desert.*
>
> LAST POEMS

This difference first struck — seized — me when I went to Oxford in the 1940s. I was studying French and supposedly solely absorbed in all that, from the Chanson de Roland to Sartre and Camus; not in peculiar English visionaries like Lawrence. Nevertheless, like many of my wartime generation, I fell on my knees with him. He said so many things we believed or didn't believe in, yet couldn't articulate; he had shocked my own parents' fuddy-duddy generation. It was obvious they were very wrong (not least, had they — and we! — but seen it, for having produced us). They'd also fathered and mothered the botched society most of us middle-class children came from. How had Lawrence (in the 1927 short story "A Dream of Life") defined it? A society full of "paltriness, smallness, meanness, fathomless ugliness, combined with a sort of chapel-going respectability!"... he was writing about Eastwood in the Midlands, where he himself had been born, but he might — give or take some minor class and cultural differences — just as convincingly have been describing the suburbs where I was born myself.

Some writers *speak* to you. They can attract, and fascinate, you may admire and envy them; yet somehow they never manage to establish the most serious writer-reader bond, which is almost a relationship like a marriage, and as closely intimate as an old friendship or love affair. By "speaking" we mean "writing" as if it may be assumed you are friends or lovers (or brothers and sisters) and so constitute a close human bond. I've been very aware of this "speaking" and being "spoken to" all my own literary life, both as reader and writer. It can take place across countless centuries, it is totally indifferent to both place and time. We use "to speak" in this somewhat odd way because of a parallel with drama. We may read *Hamlet*, written about 1600. But when we see it acted, it is now, eternally now, of the very hour we see it. "Speaking" in the novel, in this sense, destroys all other "real" time between the writing and the reading, as between the acted and the written in the theatre. It's by no means inevitably present, even in those writers who can and do sometimes "speak." It's by no means always present in Lawrence. He can write too much, can be a virulently judgmental bore, I can guess why Mencken so disliked him. But then, sometimes, one leaps to him or rather he leaps you with him, like the horse St. Mawr, to an effortlessly and infinitely higher plane, almost to another planet. Then he does "speak," here, now, in the same room. To hell with time and death, the blackshirt tyrants of our helot being: Lawrence *is*.

This speaking was what first called me to Lawrence, and is why I have always counted him as a very strong influence on my own writing, I now think a much greater one than that of the French existentialists, supposedly my favorites. "He was a part of me," in A.L. Rowse's phrase. But since the 1940s and my Oxford years, an unhappy shift of cultural mood has taken place in Britain. There were countless reasons for this change, not least the bitter experience of the two world wars and the loss of empire. Perhaps it is best labelled, broadly, as the collapse of a belief or faith in a positive life, a seemingly overwhelming need to denigrate and a fear of proving foolish if you do the opposite. It is (significantly) accompanied by a general ignorance of and indifference to nature. Satire and mockery, a comic-sour doubt of the serious (curiously similar to a trait in Jewish culture, which of course has a much longer and more painful history of suffering) has since at least the 1950s been a very acceptable attitude to take or show in England, not least among the supposedly intelligent and culturally alert. While it was directed against so many patently outmoded social and political habits and notions it was defensible, but when it began to shift to an universal disparagement . . .

Of course this oxymoronic bittersweet English culture (Keats *and* Byron, just Byron alone, for that matter) has always had a soft, romantic side as well as a hard satirical or lampoon-loving one. But the current sneer or snigger on the British face, so evident in these last thirty years, has not really been able to swallow Lawrence. He is too easy to make fun of, to mock, to put down for being so preoccupied by his own ideas, so positive all his instincts — intuition turned dogma — must be right. I can hardly blame the denigrators. Swept on in the general flood of carping, I have implicitly denied him myself (and *to* myself) for decades. I was stupidly wrong, but surely that snigger, that too fastidious (too distorted by the *Zeitgeist*) dismissal wasn't therefore right. Aspects of Lawrence, especially in those last years, do remain near impossible to defend or justify, indeed sometimes near the ridiculous. It is the ones that don't that we tend — if not positively try — to forget.

There are now countless critical and biographical accounts of Lawrence, and it is not my job — nor my wish — to ape an academic. I am a fellow-novelist and feel a frequent sympathy and admiration for him; not a scholar-critic, desperate to amass new facts and make definitive judgments. It's not that I scorn all critics, but I know the enormous gulf between creating and judging, which has nothing — or very little — to do with comparative knowledges or intelligences, but far more with possessing a kind of religiousness . . . not just the need to teach, but to express one's finer self through teaching.

Briefly, Lawrence first saw the Mexicos, both old and new, in 1922. Some three years later in 1925 he fell seriously ill there with influenza and malaria, and his tuberculosis was confirmed. At the end of that year he moved —it was to prove forever —back to Europe. In that last lustrum of his life —he was to die in 1930 —his final spirit hardened and took shape. Again and again he tried to net the butterfly ("Farewell, farewell, lost soul!") less seen than sensed. What happens to us after death? With that was bound up another great issue. Why was humanity so ubiquitously sick, in a psychic equivalent of his own wretched state of health? It was his numerous plunges into these two dark worlds, trespassing on those of anthropology and theology, philosophy and metaphysics, to say nothing of that of politics, that were to cause the trouble. Bertrand Russell thought Lawrence led directly to the Nazis; and some of what he wrote in this period can be taken (especially if one suffers from tunnel vision and over-literalism) as highly offensive to many *now* (sixty years later) widely held views on matters like fascism, racism, and feminism.

During Easter, 1927, Lawrence and his American friend Earl Brewster, passing a shopwindow in Volterra, Italy, had seen a toy white cock escaping from an egg. Brewster suggested it presented both a potential title and the chance to broach the theme of resurrection. He knew he was sowing a seed in fertile ground, for they were in Volterra gathering material for *Etruscan Places* (which devotes a chapter to the little town and their visit). The old culture was already deeply attracting Lawrence. "The Etruscan religion is concerned with all those physical and creative powers and forces which go to the building up and the destroying of the soul: the soul, the personality, being that which gradually is produced out of chaos, like a flower, only to disappear again into chaos, or the underworld. We, on the contrary, say: In the beginning was the Word! —and deny the physical universe true existence. We exist only in the Word, which is beaten out thin to cover, gild, and hide all things."

A result of this incident was the first part of the present work, called *The Escaped Cock*. It was first published in *Forum* in February, 1928. A further part, written that

93

same year, was then added to the first and the whole published, still under the same title, by the Crosbys at the Black Sun Press in Paris in September, 1929. Lawrence always preferred his own original title, and never authorized *The Man Who Died* (though he had "reluctantly" passed *The Man Who Had Died* for an abortive London edition). A first public edition in Britain under the new title appeared from Martin Secker in March, 1931; a first American, from Alfred Knopf, six months later. The complex story of the various manuscripts and typescripts of the two parts and their publication is told at length by Gerald M. Lacy in the Black Sparrow Press edition of *The Escaped Cock* (Los Angeles, 1973), and also, more simply, in Keith Sagar's introduction to Lawrence's *Complete Short Novels* (Penguin, 1982).

Almost everything he wrote in the later 1920s throws light on this austere last novel, but of especial value must be the *Last Poems* and *Apocalypse*, respectively posthumously published in 1931 and 1932. An article "The Risen Lord," first printed in 1929, may be read now in *Phoenix II*. Sagar felt this was so pertinent that it constituted almost a third of the novel. Of lesser but obvious value is *Etruscan Places*, first published in 1932, and *St. Mawr* of 1925. This last was also about a resurrection of a kind, and is, to my mind, among the very best of Lawrence's last fictions. I have just read it "in tandem" with *The Man Who Died*, and can vouch for their closeness; though one is almost sweet sherry to the other's *eau-de-vie*. *The Man* is very near a sermon; *St. Mawr* remains a brilliant short novel.

There is no doubt how highly Lawrence himself valued *The Man Who Died*, whatever his feelings might have been over the title. Several letters stress its importance. After his various brushes with the police since the 1914-18 War, and most notoriously over *Lady Chatterley's Lover*, to a sick man it must at the very least have threatened still more trouble. Christ is shown resurrected and sexually potent ("I am risen"—how dare he make such an abominable pun on one of our most sacred mysteries!). He doesn't even discreetly couple, as any decent Anglo-Saxon should, with a respectable Christian woman; but flaunts his manhood with the mere priestess of some pagan cult, a shameless foreigner.

Today, these sixty-two profoundly changed and changing years later, surely only the most bigoted and least imaginative could feel outraged. Anyone above that miserable level will understand that his rejection of his early nonconformist chapel upbringing was far more based on social and aesthetic matters than narrow sectarian ones. Lawrence asserted again and again that he was religious, indeed deeply respected Christ, at least symbolically, even if he couldn't accept much of what the church and theology had made of him . . . and insisted that all their faithful sheep must believe. In the last few decades we have perpetrated (and continue) quite enough only too real secular and biological crimes to make whatever blasphemy there is in *The Man Who Died* seem very mild indeed.

I am in Lawrence's case myself—having for years publicly called myself an atheist. As I said, in terms of all established religion (and most politics), I am so, with no belief whatever in either a personal afterlife or an intervening deity. To old-style believers, the world of people like myself may seem incredibly bleak. But it isn't. For a start our beliefs oblige us to put all reward for living —all its aesthetic point and ethical purpose, all its joys and all its duties —into life itself; and then we sometimes know, as we claim ourselves atheists, that we may also be religious —but can't say so because the word is so often assumed to be a synonym for Christian. Lawrence transparently sensed this seeming paradox, I believe, more acutely than any other writer of this century.

There are many eye-witness accounts (such as Cynthia Asquith's) of the almost palpable charge of life-energy he seemed to exude. He was "preternaturally alive," there was an "electric elemental quality that gave him a flickering radiance." He was *different* from other people, and not just in degree, but in kind.

What he intensely prized was this acute awareness of being, a sensitivity like that of a Geiger counter aroused or evoked by and in all that existed, though most strongly in simple nature and the primitive worlds remotest from high culture: that is (we lack an exact word for it), the ability to feel and venerate the *existingness* in things. It isn't quite the same as Duns Scotus's medieval haecceity (Gerard Manley Hopkins's "thisness"), the separate individuality in all things; but much more a fundamental intuitive sense of their being. Of course we humans all imagine we

95

have this sense; we know we're alive. But much of Lawrence's hatred of the cold, "over-civilized" north — not least of England and North America — stemmed precisely from his feeling that we very largely lacked any true apprehension of this existingness, indeed behaved as if we couldn't believe it there. We might have faint intimations of such a sensitivity, but we didn't, like him, profoundly treasure both it and all that provokes it. We couldn't or we wouldn't have allowed a perverted Christianity and our maniacal pursuit of the Devil — or Mammon — and the lethally soulless machine ("Man invented the machine so now the machine has invented the man") to so grossly distort our societies and our psyches. One of his best-known attempts to convey existingness was in the short story "Sun," which also belongs to this last period and to his final return to Europe and his beloved Mediterranean.

I very much doubt if I fully understood the implications of realizing this existingness when I first fell for Lawrence. I did share it, though but as a candle to his sun. It is why I became a natural historian; it is why I became a writer myself, always stumbling, despite being a novelist, after the poem; why I constantly declare myself an atheist, yet remain endlessly fascinated by religion, even by sects as remote as the Shakers; it is why, though also calling myself a French existentialist, I could never accept *le néant* and *la nausée* as one was supposed in those long-past years. Above all it's the existingness of things that has for me invariably dulled and diminished their other much more obvious qualities and importances: their beauty, their social and political significance, their moral aspects . . . all have been thrown into shadow by the dazzling revelation, like some all-changing nuclear flash, that what they are or purport to be means far, far less than that they exist.

I may speak of it as if all this were (it does so seem with Lawrence) some sort of innate gift, like a musical or a color sense or one of balance. Undoubtedly it is so in part; but I very strongly believe that it is also something that can be acquired, can be learnt and practiced, the susceptibility to it increased. At any rate I am sure that the manifold manners of life most of us have given ourselves (or more often, that society gives us) are deeply hostile and inimical to this sense of existingness. Almost all our social cultures clearly see it as a threat. Our philosophies and religions, our pleasures and pastimes, both our cultural and commoner routines and habits . . .

it is almost as if they are deliberately (devilishly!) designed to blur and obscure the fact that I exist—or better, that the "I" exists; and that this "I" is on his or her one and only brief "holiday" from an eternity of oblivion, the *néant* of the existentialists. To begin to know, so that you may fully accept, this—put most simply, that you both live and must die—is shattering, not least because it makes the apparent complete absence of any knowledge or acceptance of it in our societies incomprehensible. Why on earth do we, how can we, remain so ineffably stupid?

It was his acute and often raging horror at the insanely blind folly of humankind, especially of its more fortunate and better educated, and their total failure to see the reality of their situation, that must be seen as the constant drive behind Lawrence through most of his adult life. It was exacerbated by the 1914-18 War, but truly burst out in his last decade. It is what gave him his incredible, almost supranatural energy. The less familiar with his work sometimes shrug it off as mere egotistical vanity. It was not. It was his essence.

Against the supposed awful pessimism of us atheists over the nature of the after-life must be set Lawrence's recurrent notion of the "strange flowers such as my life has not brought forth before, new blossoms of me." These "flowers" make up much of the *Last Poems:* in effect they assert that there is an afterlife for the soul, though not for the me, the individual ego. God breaks the loathsome, self-important ego down to His own oblivion, but then finally sends a soul forth to take its place, a new man on a new morning. Lawrence, of course, cannot be read for strict common sense, narrow science or reason; but we may go to him for feeling. Feeling is what bursts through again and again in the numerous quasi-mantras of the *Last Poems*. He somehow can't really believe, because he can't feel (as he might feel a pin-prick) that what he is will one day die.

So much of the last work was written at a near white heat that language is put under the deepest strain. There is perpetual war between an intellectual and a feeling Lawrence, between the someone who "wants out" (who asks nothing, in his own words, "except to be left, in the last resort, alone, quite alone") and the lifelong egocentric. He may conceive of an afterlife in oblivion – the great goal in "The Ship of Death" – since it submerged

> *the obscene ego*
> *a grey void thing that goes without wandering*
> *a machine that in itself is nothing*
> *a centre of the evil world-soul.*

He may invite the annihilation of his own ego, yet somehow, so strong was – and remains, in this lower, latter world! – his personality, his own residual self, that his eager self-immolation is never totally credible.

> *but in the great spaces of death*
> *the winds of the afterwards kiss us into blossom*
> *of manhood.*

Like Lawrence, in such matters most of us rate feeling well above reason. We wander in a mist of vaguely "religious" prejudices, of notions imbibed in childhood. It is like looking at the outside world through smeared glass, and sometimes we can barely see it. The effort of seeing it, of (in the current jargon) deconstructing it, is too much for most of us; I suspect less through lack of knowledge or intelligence, but from a fear or dislike of having to face reality. Lawrence sensed this. It is one major reason he increasingly abandoned the (to him) flimsy froth of the more orthodox novel, and preferred to express himself (since he believed all his life that the novelist was superior to the poet, the philosopher, and the saint) in what was, for the previous admirers of his realism, a near symbolic fiction. Even though what Lawrence always called *The Escaped Cock* was set in the Mediterranean, its techniques may seem as bare, if not barren, as a New Mexican or Arizonan desert. In all this very last work he is repeatedly hammering nails, or one great nail, home. He hardly writes to please, he writes to teach through symbols. In short, he writes to parable.

All his life, ever since the days of the Pagans group at Eastwood in England and the pipedream of his ideal colony, Rananim, with its echoes of Coleridge and Southey's Pantisocracy, Lawrence had evolved a faith: the purpose of the novel was to teach.

It was didactic, moral; never to merely amuse nor simply entertain. In the *Fantasia of the Unconscious* (published in 1922, just before he began *The Plumed Serpent*) he was declaring that "for the mass of the people knowledge must be symbolical, mythical, dynamic." This required "a higher, responsible, conscious class" — the Lawrences of this world — to present and produce what the lower classes might absorb and learn from. As so often Lawrence risked at best inconsistency, having so long damned modern civilization and education, and at worst the menacing tar-brush of fascism. But the underlying signal is clear. In *The Man Who Died* Lawrence was not concerned to demonstrate what he had so often proven: that he could write fine and beautiful near-realistic novels. *The Plumed Serpent* of 1926 had come from the impact of New Mexico and his sense of his own "decayed Christianity"; but it had also come from an old self, which hadn't fully recognized the intense, burning-rapid development of the new Lawrence in the cold arms of death. I suspect this is why like most I count it a failure.

The new self needed the starkness and simplicity of *The Man Who Died*, *Apocalypse*, and the *Last Poems*, almost as Beethoven needed the sublimities of certain passages in the last quartets and piano sonatas. *The Plumed Serpent* hadn't made it clear enough what was wrong with Christianity, its placing far too much stress on the Christ-Child and, especially since the 1914-18 War, the Christ Crucified; and not nearly enough on what was for Lawrence the essential, the Christ Reborn. In *Apocalyspe* he further placed the blame for the misleading of man and the corruption of true Christianity on the Revelation of St. John of Patmos. In Richard Aldington's 1931 introduction to the book, explaining the hostility of many intellectuals, he says, "Lawrence's fundamental heresy was simply that he placed quality of feelings, intensity of sensations and passion before intellect. In this he is the very antithesis of Bernard Shaw. . . ."

Needless to say this novel is not faultless. There's always a danger in using euphe-misms. Personally I in general prefer them to the careless crudity of so much contemporary would-be realism, but their drawback is that they can, and with time only too often do, pratfall into unintended humor. Every novelist knows the prob-lem of sex: who will your words please, who will they offend? The woman-flows (*not* menstruation!), the new suns coming up, the intricate warm roses, the shutting and stirring lotuses, the scars and buds . . . they don't always present Lawrence at his happiest.

Nor does the element that has upset so many women in recent years . . . and I think quite rightly: his often rather painfully obtrusive masculinism-phallicism. This aspect of Lawrence, like his rashes of anti-Semitism, is not acceptable to many of us since the Holocaust and the rise of the feminist movement. Yet I believe the virtues of both his writing and his personality enormously exceed the black shadows of these familiar bees in his bonnet. Lawrence is not quasi-divinely perfect, and we can't make him so.

One of those virtues is to my mind the way he finds such a simple, sometimes near Biblical, style to tell his story. The occasional flashes of his old poetry show a last relic of his acute powers of existingness; old feeling infuses skilled imagining. There is that always fertile pithiness; that flair for the striking phrase (what an asset he would have proved on Madison Avenue): "words beget words, even as gnats," "the dread insomnia of compulsion," "the sheer stillness of the inner life," and many others.

I have never been able to read Lawrence for long before being plunged, besides the sympathy and affection (and pepper-grains of irritation), into thought. Part of his hyper-awareness, his existingness, his soul-energy is that he seems also a mirror for the reader. You must start searching for yourself in his texts. *The Man Who Died* needs to be read by someone fully aware of the despairing, almost hectic seriousness with which Lawrence saw mankind's deep-rooted psychological and emotional problems. Those last are what this text is essentially about, not the precise rightness or wrongness of its views concerning Christ. The human side of the world, *our* world, is very sick, and has become several times worse since Lawrence himself died; and I believe we need, desperately, whatever our own religious beliefs, to listen to his message. He isn't trying to shock us; but passionately, like all good preachers, to save us.

I'd like to finish with two quotations, the one from Richard Aldington's introduction to *Apocalypse;* and the other from the very last page of *Apocalypse* itself, which gives both his living mind and his living soul.

"I shall only say a little about *The Man Who Died*. It is intensely personal, and the saddest thing Lawrence ever wrote. It is the only thing in his work which looks like a confession of defeat, and this he promptly countered by writing *Apocalypse*. The opening part when he describes the mingled agony and gradual happiness in creeping back from death to life is full of pathos; one can't help thinking of his own sufferings as he recovered from one or other of his serious crises. Like much of Lawrence's writing, it has more than one meaning. You can take it as an expression of his latest feelings about Jesus — a rejection of Jesus as a teacher, an acceptance of Jesus as the lover. The mistake of Jesus was not in loving, but in trying to influence men by a doctrine of love. Even when he was struggling with the problem of love and hatred, Lawrence was always a great lover; his deepest and most passionate belief was in love."

Now Lawrence. "What man most passionately wants is his living wholeness and his living unison, not his own isolate salvation of his 'soul'. Man wants his physical fulfilment first and foremost, since now, once and once only, he is in the flesh and potent. For man, the vast marvel is to be alive. For man, as for flower and beast and bird, the supreme triumph is to be most vividly, most perfectly alive. Whatever the unborn and the dead may know, they cannot know the beauty, the marvel of being alive in the flesh. The dead may look after the afterwards. But the magnificent here and now of life in the flesh is ours, and ours alone, and ours only for a time. We ought to dance with rapture that we should be alive and in the flesh, and part of the living, incarnate cosmos."

JOHN FOWLES

This book, the seventeenth issued with this imprint,
was designed by and printed for James and Carolyn Robertson
at The Yolla Bolly Press, Covelo, California, during the summer and
fall of 1992. The illustrations were drawn and cut in wood by
Leonard Baskin. The book was composed in the Bembo types.
The text and illustrations were printed by Aaron Johnson at the Press,
using mould-formed Somerset paper, imported from England.
Endsheets for the edition were handmade at the Twinrocker Paper
Mill in Brookston, Indiana. The edition is one hundred thirty copies,
of which one hundred are offered for sale. Thirty-five copies
have been bound in vellum at the Press by Renee Menge,
are accompanied by a suite of unbound signed prints, and are
enclosed in a box of bay laurel and cedar woods. Of these, copies
numbered 1 to 30 are for sale. Eighty-five copies are bound in a cover
of Japanese cotton over boards and are enclosed in a linen slipcase.
Of these, copies numbered 31 to 90 are for sale. Ten unsigned
and unbound copies are available for sale to bookbinders.
All other copies are reserved for the artist and the Press.